THE REAL THING

Brian Falkner was born and raised in Auckland, New Zealand. He has worked as a radio journalist, radio announcer, graphic designer and internet developer. He has also written several novels for children including *The Real Thing*, *The Flea Thing* and *The Super Freak*, all of which are set in Glenfield High School. He lives on the North Shore of Auckland.

THE
REAL
THING

BRIAN FALKNER

**WALKER
BOOKS**

This is a work of fiction. Names, characters, places and incidents are either the product of the author's imagination or, if real, are used fictitiously.

First published in Great Britain 2008 by Walker Books Ltd
87 Vauxhall Walk, London SE11 5HJ

Published by arrangement with Mallinson Rendel Publishers, New Zealand

2 4 6 8 10 9 7 5 3 1

Text © 2004 Brian Falkner
Cover design by Walker Books Ltd

The right of Brian Falkner to be identified as author of this work has been asserted by him in accordance with the Copyright, Designs and Patents Act 1988

This book has been typeset in Minion Regular

Printed and bound in Great Britain by J.H. Haynes & Co. Ltd

British Library Cataloguing in Publication Data:
a catalogue record for this book is available from the British Library

ISBN 978-1-4063-1238-6

www.walkerbooks.co.uk

CONTENTS

FOREWORD

Parts of this book are based on fact; other parts are pure fiction. The secret formula of Coca-Cola, for example, is indeed a secret and The Coca-Cola Company is steadfast in its silence over the recipe. The rule about only three people knowing the formula at any one time is a part of the Coca-Cola legend, as is the rule that the three cannot travel on the same aeroplane, although the legend differs in the number of people who know the recipe, depending on where you heard it.

The description of The Coca-Cola Company headquarters is for the most part accurate, as is its location in Coca-Cola Plaza, Atlanta. The mixing process, and the sweeteners used, are documented fact.

While the characters are all fictional, several of them have the names of real people. These were the winners of a number of competitions held in primary and intermediate schools around New Zealand. Congratulations to Hamish Knox, Kelly Fraser, Mohammad Sarrafzadeh, Keelan McCafferty, and Kate Fogarty, whose names all appear in this book.

The Coca-Cola Company does not endorse the contents of this book.

For Ann, Laura and Emma, who know why.

THE TASTE TEST

There's something very special about a school fair. It's the excitement of the weeks building up to it, and all the work that the kids do in the classroom, painting posters and making signs. It's the colour and the bustle of the day itself, and how it always seems to be sunny, and the fact that on school fair day all the rules about what you're allowed to eat, and not to eat, go straight out the window, and you're allowed to stuff yourself with toffee apples, followed by candy floss, followed by hot dogs, followed by hot chips, followed by whatever else you want, followed by as much fizzy drink as you can drink!

Which brings us, in a roundabout kind of way, to Fizzer.

Fizzer Boyd was blessed with E.S.P. Not Extra-Sensory-Perception, like the amazing Kreskin, or Uri Geller, or any of those frauds on the TV who claim to have psychic powers. Fizzer couldn't bend spoons, or move things with his mind, or read your thoughts, or tell the future (however, he did have good intuition, but we'll get to that). What Fizzer had was *Extraordinary* Sensory Perception, although he insisted that it was nothing unusual and that he had just trained himself to be that way.

Where his friends would see a small dot in the sky, Fizzer could tell you what kind of bird it was. When they did the eyesight tests to see if you needed glasses, Fizzer would read the name of the printer off the fine print at the bottom of the eye chart. He could hear footsteps at the end of the corridor before anybody else, and he would know from the sound if it was their teacher returning so they should all stop talking and get on with their assignments. When the First Fifteen came back from an away game he'd know who they'd played by the smell of the mud on their boots. Touch a leaf to the back of his neck, and he could feel what kind of tree it came from.

Fizzer insisted that anyone could do this. That it was just a matter of patience and focus. That you had to narrow your perception down to just the single sense you were using, instead of relying on all five. He said that was why blind people often had extraordinary hearing, and deaf people could read lips flapping at high speed a hundred metres away.

Sight, sound, touch, smell, Fizzer was amazing at them all. But the sense he was most well-known for – that he became world-famous for – was his sense of taste.

And that's also why Jason, Flea and Tupai were all perched around him on a stand at the Glenfield School Fair.

Fizzer's real name was Fraser, but everybody called him Fizzer because he could do this clever trick with fizzy drinks.

Give him a sip of a fizzy drink, any fizzy drink, and he could tell you what it was. He could tell Coca-Cola from Pepsi (although everyone could do that). But Fizzer could tell Diet Coke from normal Coke, he could tell Coke-out-of-a-can from Coke-out-of-a-bottle. He could even tell the difference between Coke from a two-litre bottle and Coke from a 1.25 litre bottle, as long as it was fresh.

So Fizzer had his own stand at the school fair. There was a

hundred-dollar prize for anyone who could produce a can or a bottle of soft drink that Fizzer couldn't identify.

It had been Tupai's idea and he was quite proud of it. They charged a dollar a go and, with the huge prize money, they had lots and lots of entries. It had been Jason's idea to set up a soft-drink stand in the next alley because, he figured, they had to get their soft drink from somewhere …

They made money selling the soft drink, and they made money when Fizzer correctly identified the soft drink. It was quite a racket really, but it was all legal and, anyway, all the money raised went to the school swimming pool fund.

And it was all going rather nicely thank you until Jenny arrived. Tagging along after her was her boyfriend, Phil Domane.

Phil brought his own can of soft drink; a plain, standard Coca-Cola can that he'd purchased at the local dairy on his way to the fair.

There were certain rules to the game. Flea and Jason had to check each drink first to make sure it was a legitimate soft drink and that it hadn't been tampered with. Tupai, the strongest kid in the school, stood around with his arms crossed, looking like a bouncer, in case there were any arguments.

They checked Phil's can carefully and poured a little into a paper cup for Fizzer. (It had to be paper, he said, because he could taste the plastic ones.)

Phil put his money down and sat in the folding chair they had set up in front of the stand while Fizzer went through his little act. This was going to be easy, Tupai thought. Coca-Cola in a can. Fizzer would identify that in a second.

Fizzer waved his hand around the top of the paper cup, drawing the aroma of the drink into his nostrils. He swirled the drink, watching the liquid flow around inside the cup and the way the bubbles broke to the surface. He held the cup to his ear and listened to the tiny fizzing sound.

Mostly that was just for show, part of his act. He could tell the drink in a couple of seconds simply by drinking it, but that didn't look impressive enough for the punters, so he went through the whole rigmarole each time.

Phil waited patiently, Flea and Jason lined up the next contestant, and Tupai stood still and looked like a bouncer, while Fizzer eventually put the cup to his lips.

There was a pause, which was normal, but it went on for five or six seconds, which was not.

Flea and Jason both stopped what they were doing and turned to watch Fizzer. Still not worried though, surely he could tell Coca-Cola!

Phil waited some more. He didn't look concerned. He was expecting to lose. He was helping support the stand.

Fizzer was still silent, and then Tupai started to get worried. Had something gone wrong? Was the cup not clean? Actually it was clean, fresh from the stack of new cups.

Finally Fizzer said, obviously uncertain for the very first time, 'Corker Cola?'

Corker Cola was an Australian brand, just a cheap rip-off of the *real thing*: Coca-Cola.

Phil looked up in surprise.

'No, no, it's "Ice Cola",' Fizzer said quickly, but the expression on Phil's face told him he was wrong.

Phil looked at Tupai, and a few moments later, more than a little stunned, Tupai handed him the hundred-dollar note that they had pinned to the top of the stand.

'Congratulations, Phil,' said Flea, who didn't like Phil, but was big-hearted enough to be polite.

'I … er … thanks?' Phil stuttered.

Fizzer looked heart-broken, maybe from having been wrong, or maybe at losing the entire day's profits from the stand.

'What was it?' he asked.

Jason silently showed him the can.

Fizzer shook his head. 'No way. Not sweet enough. That was a little … well … not quite bitter, but Coke is definitely sweeter than that.'

Flea said, 'We poured it ourselves.'

Fizzer snatched the can away from Flea, angry with himself, not his friends. He sniffed at the can and then drank some more, straight from the can.

'This is not Coke,' he said.

Jason insisted, 'I opened the can myself, and it hadn't been tampered with.'

Fizzer glared at Phil, who shrugged as if innocent of all charges and said, 'Don't ask me. I just bought it at the dairy.'

Fizzer looked back at the can, then back at Phil.

'Which dairy?' he asked.

'The corner dairy.'

So they packed up the whole stand there and then, and the lot of them, except for Jenny and Phil, headed off for the corner dairy.

And they never did get to have any candyfloss, or toffee apples, or hot-dogs, or hot chips.

They drank all the fizzy drink left over though.

THE EXECUTIVES

At exactly that moment, in the cabin of a Lear Jet, thousands of miles away from their school, events were happening that would change all of their lives.

Actually, it may not have been at the exact same moment, what with international time zones and everything, but it sounds better that way.

Mr Bingham Elderoy Statham the Third – although he never used the 'Third' except on official stationery, because he thought it made him sound like a fraction – was quite comfortably seated in the soft leather lounge chair in the pleasantly appointed cabin of the jet.

It was a company jet. The company that he worked for – and had a substantial share-holding in – was one of the largest companies in the world, so it could afford a company jet, or two, or three. In fact it had a small fleet. The company that Bingham (Bing to his friends) Statham worked for had branches in almost every country of the world. It only sold a few products, but its flagship product was as American as Mickey Mouse or the Statue of Liberty.

Bingham Statham worked for The Coca-Cola Company, and he was quite worried that afternoon (it was afternoon where he was in the world, which happened to be Los Angeles) about two separate things. The first thing was that his ferret had died. He had two pet ferrets, named Olivia and Candy, after his first two wives (which annoyed Margie, his third wife, to distraction). Only now Candy had died, of unknown causes, and he was worried about Olivia. Worried that she might contract the same illness, and worried that she would be pining for her friend. Ferrets are very social creatures, and he felt she would miss Candy terribly.

The second reason he was worried was that the jet seemed to be flying in the wrong direction. Candy – the second wife, not the ferret – always said he had a good sense of direction. But that sense of direction said he was going the wrong way.

He was supposed to be flying to New Jersey for an important meeting with Maxim Portugale of Stepan Co., the people who imported the specially treated coca leaves that were used to produce the secret Coca-Cola formula.

Ralph Alderney Winkler (the First) was flying to the same meeting.

Both he and Bingham were flying from LA, where they had been at a conference of Important American Business Leaders (IABL), at roughly the same time, and there were three spare lounge chairs, plus a small soft sofa, on the Lear Jet. Yet Ralph Alderney Winkler was not flying with Bingham. He was on a commercial flight. First class of course, but still a step down for Mr Winkler, who was accustomed to only the utmost luxury at all times. A bit like Olivia (the wife not the ferret).

The reason was that Bingham and Ralph were two of only three people in the world who knew the secret formula to the world's most popular soft drink: Coca-Cola. There was a scientist living in Okinawa off the coast of Japan who claimed he'd worked it out, but The Coca-Cola Company denied this, and the scientist had no way of proving his formula was correct.

The Coca-Cola Company has its own laws, commandments you could call them, and one of them is this: the three people who know the recipe at any one time are never allowed to travel together, whether it is by limousine, boat, helicopter, fast camel or Lear Jet. The reason is obvious. If some terrible accident occurred and all three were lost, then the secret formula of Coca-Cola, and countless millions of dollars of company profits, would be lost with them.

There was another Lear Jet that was supposed to have taken Ralph Winkler, but a fault had developed with one of its engines, so it had to go for a maintenance check and was unavailable for the flight.

Which was why Ralph Alderney Winkler was sitting in a first class seat, on a Boeing 727, probably no more than a few kilometres from Bingham Statham in his soft leather lounge chair in the cabin of the Lear.

The third person with knowledge of the recipe was Ms Clara Fogsworth, an elderly spinsterish lady with gold-rimmed glasses and a heart to match, who was currently fly-fishing in the Bahamas.

Spinsterish she may have been, but a spinster she was not. She had buried one husband and still led a very active and exciting life despite her advancing years.

But back to Bingham, Bing, we should call him because we know him so well by now that we are almost friends.

He alternated worrying about Olivia, the surviving ferret,

with worrying about why the plane was heading sou'west, instead of sou'east.

The pilot had been in to see him before take-off, as was considered polite, and he seemed a nice enough young man. Not one of the pilots that Bing recognised, but then there were a lot of them, and they changed quite regularly, so he didn't know all of them by sight, not by any means.

After a while, though, the worry about the plane started to take over from the worry about the ferret, and he unbuckled his seat belt and wandered carefully forward to the closed cockpit door. It was locked, which was a little unusual, so he knocked.

There was no answer, so he rapped a little louder. Still no response. So he called out, 'Hello. Excuse me, pilot.'

Still nothing. As he made his way back to his seat, the thought slowly crossed his mind that maybe he had been kidnapped.

Ms Clara Fogsworth knew she had been kidnapped. There was no doubt in her mind. Either that or she was on her way to a very unusual surprise birthday party. However, it wasn't her birthday, and, even if it was, she doubted she would have been roughed up to the degree that she had been by the two thugs who had greeted her as she walked off the boat.

'Roughed up' is a relative term, which means different things to different people.

To Clara Fogsworth, the stern hand on her upper arm that had steered her firmly, but courteously, towards a waiting black van, had been the roughest treatment she had experienced in her life. Unforgivable, she thought. How could they?

How could he?!! she thought, with a double exclamation mark.

He being Mr Joseph Sturdee, a handsome, athletic man she had been dating for about three months. He was young too, only fifty-five, with the most devilish grin which made her go quite weak at the knees. Of his involvement in the kidnapping she had no doubt: he had led her straight into the hands, the *rough* hands, of the thugs.

That raised the horrible possibility of the whole three-month long romance being nothing but a set up. Ms Clara Fogsworth didn't like to think about that too much though, because the whole affair had been quite a boost to her ego. He was, after all, a tall, handsome and *younger* man.

But, nevertheless, here she was, with her hands now tied in front of her with one of those dreadful, cheap plastic ties they use to tie up plants, sitting in the back of a black van with no windows, speeding to some unknown place somewhere in the Bahamas.

Rough treatment indeed!

In New Jersey, not all that much later, Ralph Winkler eased himself into the back of a long, black limousine. Not as comfortable as usual he thought, looking with disdain at the plain cloth upholstery. After having to endure first class service on the flight from LA, he really felt he should at least have had suede or leather seating in the limousine.

'You're from Stepan Co.?' he asked the large man who squeezed in beside him, intending to complain.

The man nodded, but he can't have been, or he wouldn't have pulled that canvas bag down over Ralph Alderney Winkler's head.

BOJUTSU

Fizzer was into Eastern Mysticism, and that's how he got through those next two weeks. His dad said it was just a phase, the Eastern Mysticism, and he was probably right, but, true or not, Fizzer threw himself whole-heartedly into his meditation, yoga and martial arts training to take his mind off the catastrophe.

And it really was a catastrophe. It might seem like a small thing, getting a brand of soft drink wrong but it brought Fizzer's world crashing down around his tastebuds. Everything he believed in, everything he told others about focus and perception and training, it was all gone. Just because he couldn't tell one can of cola from another.

They'd gone back to the corner dairy and bought another can of Coke, except Fizzer said that it wasn't Coke either. Mr Lim, the dairy owner, wouldn't have a bar of that though. He said he just sold the stuff, he didn't put it in the cans, and he didn't care too much because Fizzer kept buying another can, taking one sip, and saying, 'That's not Coke either.'

As long as he kept paying for the cans, it was fine by Mr Lim.

Fizzer's friends all rallied around and tried to support him as best they could, because he was their buddy, he was their mate, and they knew he was really distressed.

Jenny even joined Fizzer's karate school, or dojo as they called it. She said it was for self-defence, and that was true, but, just as much, it was about simply being a friend. For some reason Jenny felt a bit guilty about what had happened, although it wasn't her fault at all. It wasn't even Phil's fault.

Flea joined up at the karate dojo too, but he had reasons of his own. Flea used to go out with Jenny before Phil did, and he never totally got over her. Once Flea and Jenny had joined the dojo, Phil had to as well, just to keep an eye on Jenny and Flea. Which only went to show that he didn't know Jenny half as well as he thought he did.

Tupai went along to watch a few times, although karate wasn't really his scene. He much preferred boxing and hoped to be a professional boxer one day. They even tried to talk Jason into going along but he kept making excuses and avoiding it. He wasn't much good at sports, Jason.

It was a Wednesday, seven-thirty-ish, and Tupai was sitting on the floor beside the padded mats of the dojo watching a bojutsu lesson.

CRACK! The training bo smacked down on Fizzer's padded helmet with a noise that sounded like his skull had been broken wide open. It wasn't; it was just the noise the training bo made.

A bo is a big long stick. King Arthur would have called it a stave or a staff, and it was a common English weapon in the early days. But the big difference between the Japanese martial art of bojutsu and English staff-fighting is in the moves. The English just used to whack each other around a bit, if you believe those old Robin Hood films. But the Japanese had turned it into an art form.

The difference between a fighting bo and a training bo, is that the training bo has bamboo shafts attached loosely down each side. When you hit your (heavily padded) opponent, the bamboo smacks against the side of the bo and makes that cracking sound.

CRACK! The upswing of the bo crashed up under Fizzer's arm, knocking his own bo from his grasp.

Dennis Cray, the instructor, took off his helmet and bowed to Fizzer, who bowed back before retrieving his bo and scurrying to the side of the mat, where he sat with his legs crossed like the rest of the bojutsu class.

Dennis was the teacher, the Sensei of the dojo, and possibly the toughest man alive. He was a fourth dan black belt in karate, Okinawan Goju-Ryu style, an expert in bojutsu. He held a private pilot's licence, and spent the rest of his time mountain climbing, caving, scuba diving, and he even combined the lot in a really dangerous sport called black-water diving, where he dived in underground lakes and rivers.

Dennis was due to go to Japan in a few weeks to attempt the 100 man kumite. That's a karate event where you have to fight 100 opponents one after the other, and beat at least half of them. Very few New Zealanders have even attempted it, and only one or two have succeeded.

Fizzer had been learning bojutsu for months, but it was the first time for the others. They all seemed to enjoy it, especially Flea. Even Tupai found himself wondering what it would be like to swing that big stick around his shoulders and under his arms with the incredible speed and precision that Dennis did it. Maybe he would give it a go, he thought. Maybe next month.

Fizzer enjoyed it too, but overshadowing his enjoyment was this overwhelming sense of loss. The world as he knew it had changed, and it affected everything, even the energy he put into his lesson.

Somebody had to do something, Tupai realised as he watched Fizzer, and he wished it could be him, but he had no idea what to do.

Tupai was not blessed with intuition the way Fizzer was, and sometimes laughed at him about intuition being a feminine thing. That used to annoy Fizzer a bit, who said he had read in the *Reader's Digest* an article which said that it was the 'subconscious connection of seemingly unrelated facts to form a conclusion for which there is no obvious rationale', or something along those lines.

Tupai wasn't very good at forming conclusions for which there was no obvious rationale, but he did occasionally have some good ideas of his own, without the benefit of intuition, and he had one just then. It didn't make a lot of sense, so maybe it was a kind of intuition, but, either way, he acted on it.

He slipped out of the dojo, as quietly as he could, and trotted three or four blocks down the street to the superette. He bought a couple of cans of Coke from the pretty check-out girl, and gave her a really big smile, because she was *really* pretty. She didn't look up from her till roll though, so it was wasted.

He walked back to the dojo thinking about Bruce Lee movies and pretty girls who didn't smile at you, and watched the rest of the lesson.

When the others had cleaned the floor of the dojo with their towels, which for some reason was part of the lesson, and changed out of their karate gis, they emerged one by one from the front entrance of the converted warehouse which was the dojo.

Tupai met Fizzer on the steps and, without a word, handed him one of the cans. Fizzer froze, as did the others, and Tupai's big heart stopped beating. He had been trying to help, but from the expression on Fizzer's face you would have thought he had just been handed a live grenade with the pin pulled out.

Jenny shook her head. 'Tupai, I don't think you should have …'

Fizzer cut her off. 'No, no. It's all right. It's OK, Tupai; I think I know where you're coming from. Thanks mate, but no thanks. If you know what I mean.'

Something welled up from deep inside Tupai and, without thinking about it properly, he said, 'Drink it, Fizzer, just try it.'

Fizzer looked dead at Tupai, without blinking, which is really hard to do. Jenny started to move in between them, but before she could get in the way, Fizzer reached out, took the can, snapped the top and took a long guzzle.

He looked up, and there was a spark in his eyes that they hadn't seen since the school fair. There was a lot of confusion too, but at least the spark was back.

'Now that,' he said vigorously, 'is Coca-Cola!'

AMATIL

The offices of Coca-Cola Amatil (NZ) Limited were located in a leafy side street in a bustling, industrial area in Mt Wellington, in Auckland. The head of Public Relations for the company was Harry Truman, who was absolutely no relation to the former US President who shared his name.

The PR man for Coca-Cola was Harry Seamus Truman, and the former President was Harry S. Truman (believe it or not, his middle name was 'S'), so they had exactly the same initials, but that was where the resemblance ended.

Harry Seamus Truman was from Ireland. He was tall and of slim build but strong around the shoulders because he did a lot of swimming. Not quite as much as he would have liked to do, thanks to the pressures of his job, but quite a lot all the same. He looked more like Pierce Brosnan, the actor, who also came from Ireland, than he looked like Harry Truman, the former President who didn't (come from Ireland).

Harry liked his job. He liked his office, which overlooked a small park at the rear of the building. He liked the people he worked with and the company he worked for. But he didn't always like the people he had to deal with each day, and, as the PR man for Coca-Cola, that was a lot of people.

There were advertising agency people, slickly dressed and

slickly spoken, with the latest mobile phones dangling from their ears. There were tabloid journalists, who thought there must be some dirt to dig up on the giant American corporation, and who rolled into his office reeking of cigarette smoke, and asking bizarre questions about bizarre things that there was just no answer to. Then there were sponsorship people, who wanted Coca-Cola to sponsor everything from Sea Scout troops to protest rallies for the Concerned Citizens Against Just About Everything. Sponsorship people arrived in his office in ill-fitting suits, or raw cotton shirts and roman sandals, depending on what kind of group they belonged to, and he always listened to them.

People deserved a hearing, he thought, and he always explained to them The Coca-Cola Company's strict sponsorship policy, but if, after hearing that, they still wanted to come and see him and put their case, then he always gave them the time.

As a result he worked very long hours and had far less time for swimming than he would have liked.

He couldn't work out just who was standing in his office today but, always hoping to find diamonds in the rough of human nature, he greeted the two boys warmly and invited them to sit down.

The taller of the two was growing his hair long, but wasn't there yet, Harry decided. Fraser was his name. He had an *awareness* about him, a *connection* with the space around him, as if he were intimately acquainted with every facet of the room, from the dust on the upper shelves where the cleaner could never be bothered to clean, to the cigarette burn on the carpet, concealed by a pot plant, that a journalist from the *Weekly Inquisition* had left when Harry had asked him not to smoke in his office.

It was a very strange feeling to have about someone, and Harry wondered if he perhaps shouldn't have had the double-shot cappuccino that morning.

The shorter, but more powerfully built lad, Tupai, looked like he could tear the arms off a grizzly bear if he had to, but there was a ready smile to his lips, and a cheeky personality that shone through his eyes.

On first appearances, Harry decided, he liked these two lads. But he would have to see what they wanted.

There was a brief exchange of pleasantries, mainly about the weather and the rugby league games scheduled for that weekend. Then, without further preamble, Fraser brought two unopened cans of Coke out of a small backpack and plonked them on the table before him.

He looked at Harry and, with a very serious expression, said, 'You have a problem in one of your factories.'

Harry started to protest but stopped himself, deciding to give the lad the benefit of the doubt. They had made a good first impression after all.

Fraser took a couple of empty cans out of the backpack and showed the batch numbers on the bottom of the cans and explained dates and described what he thought was wrong with the drink.

'Not enough sugar,' he said. 'It's not sweet enough.' Then the boy with the not-quite-long hair stared Harry straight in the eye and said, 'If I had to guess, I'd say it's down about fifteen percent.'

Harry let him finish, then took a deep breath. He liked this kid. He had two teenagers of his own, and the only thing they were interested in was playing computer games on a console in front of the television. The thought of them getting off their backsides and making a trip across town because they thought a can of Coke had *fifteen percent* less sugar than it should have was so unthinkable that there wasn't even a word for it.

'Where do you live?' Harry asked.

'Glenfield,' Fraser replied.

'That must be four bus trips from here.'

The other lad spoke up then, the natural smile curling from his face. 'Only three.'

Only three bus rides. These boys had taken three buses to tell Harry Truman, the PR man from Ireland, that something was wrong with a can of Coke. The sad thing was they were almost certainly wrong.

Most people would have politely shown them the door at this stage, but Harry could only think of his own two boys and sigh. He decided then and there, that for the effort they had put in, they deserved an effort in return.

'We have very highly paid people who do nothing all day long but make sure our product is perfect,' he said. 'They're called Quality Control Inspectors. The machines that mix the drinks are worth millions of dollars. It is inconceivable that the Coke could be wrong. I'm sorry but I just can't accept it.'

Fraser said simply, 'Try it yourself,' as Tupai produced, almost by magic, two paper cups and placed them on the table in front of him. They made a good double act, Harry thought.

Fraser poured a little of the first can into one cup and a little of the other can into the other cup. Harry stared at him for a little while.

'OK, OK, I'll take the test,' he smiled at last.

He tried the first drink; the one Fraser said was all right. It tasted like Coca-Cola should. He tried the second, and that tasted fine too.

'No difference,' he said, a little sadly for their sake.

'Taste it,' Fraser said.

'I just did.'

'No, *really* taste it, what's left in your mouth, concentrate on it. Shut your eyes if you have to.'

This was starting to get a little silly, but once started …

Harry shut his eyes and concentrated, and damned if he couldn't almost see what the boy was talking about. Confused, he tried the first cup again, then the second. Again there was just the faintest feeling that the second was not quite as sweet as the first.

Thoughtfully he picked up the cans and looked again at the batch numbers.

'Different production lines,' he said carefully. 'I'm not saying you're right, but just for interest, and as I have no other appointments this morning, let's go for a little walk.'

Harry quickly emailed his secretary to cancel the rest of his appointments for the morning, which included two advertising agencies, one journalist from the *Conspirer*, and a group from the *Save the Paper Wasp* foundation.

A few moments later, wearing 'Visitor' badges and funny plastic shower caps over their heads, they were walking through the massive barn-like structure that housed the bottling and canning machines. As they walked, Harry explained a little about the five factory lines of mixing machines and the secret formula that came, already mixed, in twenty-litre drums from the factories that produced it in Puerto Rico, Africa, and the place of his birth: Ireland.

He pointed out where the water was purified, where the

mixing happened, where the carbonating happened, and was going to tell them the quite interesting fact that only three people in the whole world knew the recipe for Coke, and they weren't allowed to travel on the same plane, when they arrived at the Cobrix machine, and he didn't have time.

Kelly Fraser, the QCI for the machine, met them by the control panel, and the operator also hung around in the background wondering about the sudden attention.

'This is a Cobrix machine,' Harry said. 'There is one on every line. It constantly monitors the brix of the liquid, that's the sweetness level. This is how we make sure the mixture is exactly right.' He turned to Kelly who had an odd look on her face, part concern and part curiosity.

'This young lad thinks,' began Harry, 'this line is not mixing enough sugar in with the formula and the water.' Before Kelly could open her mouth he continued. 'And I think there's a possibility he's right.'

Then she did protest, quite vigorously too.

'It is not possible,' she spluttered, after all, her reputation was at stake. 'Look right here.'

She motioned to the boys to gather around and pointed to a digital read-out on the control panel. 'This monitors the exact sugar level as the drink is being mixed. If it dropped as much as you say, an alarm would go off here,' she indicated the alarm, 'and we'd know all about it. Look.' Everyone looked. 'The number is rock steady.'

Fraser seemed a little downcast at that, Harry noted. More than he would have expected. Can't win 'em all mate, he wanted to say.

Kelly was still staring at the read-out. 'That is a little odd,' she finally admitted.

'What?'

'Well, the machine automatically adjusts itself if there is a small drop, to maintain the correct levels. It does vary slightly, just a fraction of a percent, as it self-adjusts.'

'And?'

'It's rock steady. It's too rock steady. It should be up and down just a few fractions of a percentage point, but it's not moving at all.'

'What could cause that?' Tupai asked.

'Well, either the level just happens to be perfect at the moment, or perhaps there's a faulty sensor in the machine itself, or even a loose connection here at the control panel.'

Before she could stop him, Tupai reached over, grabbed a bunch of wires at the rear of the panel and waggled them back and forth.

'Don't do that!' she exclaimed, but far too late.

Instantly, amazingly, in front of their eyes, the numbers on the read-out dropped, quite significantly, then began flickering, up a little, down a little, just as she had described. At that moment the alarm went off with a loud chirruping sound.

'Oh. My. Gosh,' Kelly Fraser said in three short sentences. 'Start a shut-down.' This was to the operator, who looked even more confused and a little panicked.

Kelly was a model of efficiency. She pulled a radio from her belt and called in a maintenance crew even as she talked to the foreman and organised for the work-load from this production line to be shifted to other lines.

Harry just stood there and thought of his two sons and

didn't say anything. He did some calculations in his head though. He took the actual sugar level reading and subtracted it from the correct reading to get the difference. Then he multiplied that by a hundred and divided it by the correct reading. He'd come second in his class (in Ireland) at maths.

The answer came to thirteen and a half percent.

THE TURTLE DOVE

Bing Statham awoke to find himself on board a quite comfortably sized yacht, the private kind (with engines), not the sailing kind (with sails). The yacht was called the *Turtle Dove*, and you'd have to be very rich to own a boat like that.

It was well-fitted out, as they say in the boat-building industry, with plush Canadian hardwood panelling, luxurious Turkish carpets, lacy French drapes and Italian designed bunks, which were not only very fashionable, but also very comfortable. In fact, everything on board the boat was very expensive and very stylish. The only thing was, nothing really went well with anything else. The drapes and the carpet competed for your attention, the Italian bunks were at odds with the Canadian hardwood, while the bunks and the drapes just turned their backs and refused to talk to each other at all.

Bing knew none of this as he slowly emerged from quite a pleasant dream, the details of which he could not remember – but then he never could remember dreams – and threw an arm across the slender, sun-tanned shoulders of Margie Alyssa Statham the third (wife). Except she wasn't there.

Some people called Margie a trophy wife, behind his back, and whispers of that had reached his ears. He thought it was very unkind and made her sound like something he would mount on the wall in his study, next to the two stags and the black bear from his younger hunting days. And he would never do that to lovely, lively, sweet, blonde, quite-a-bit-younger-than-him Margie. Although he wouldn't have minded putting the heads of Olivia and/or Candy, his first two wives, on the wall. Particularly Candy, who had run off with the actor from that soap opera and then turned around and sued Bing for millions of dollars, *and won*!

It was cosmic justice, in Bing's mind, when the former wife of the soap opera star had then sued the cad for millions of dollars, and she had won as well. The world turned in funny ways sometimes.

But Margie, with the supermodel looks and figure, was not a trophy wife and it was quite unfair for people to say that about her. Margie loved Bing deeply, Bing knew, and he loved her back just as much.

But she wasn't there. Instead, there was this annoying deep-seated throbbing that sounded almost like the engines of a medium-sized private yacht.

With that thought all the events of the previous day came flooding back. Bing sat bolt upright in bed, cracked his head on the underside of the fashionable Italian upper bunk, and dropped back down again, rubbing his forehead and cursing in words he hadn't used since his younger hunting days.

He got up again slowly and fumbled around on the wall by the bunk until he found a light switch.

Subtle down-lights illuminated the cabin and his first thought on seeing where he was, was that whoever owned it needed a new interior decorator.

Clara Fogsworth and Ralph Winkler were seated in the comfortable, but garishly coloured lounge of the boat when he finally stumbled his way along the corridor and emerged into the room.

They looked like they were almost expecting to see him, at least they weren't at all surprised, but Bing was shocked witless to see them. So shocked in fact that the first words out of his mouth were quite inane really.

'Clara! Ralph!' he said. 'You can't be here. We're not allowed to travel on the same boat!'

Ralph rolled his eyes. It wasn't the brightest thing to say after all, but Bing *had* just bumped his head on the upper bunk.

Clara Fogsworth said politely, 'Hello Bingham.' She never called anyone by their nickname, no matter how well she knew them. She continued. 'I rather think that is the least of our worries.'

Bingham Elderoy Statham was no fool. He hadn't become a millionaire by being a fool, and he certainly hadn't got his seat on the board of directors of The Coca-Cola Company by being a fool. But, even so, it took him a few moments to put it all together in his mind.

'We've all been kidnapped,' he said, and then he realised. 'They want the secret formula to Coca-Cola!'

'I'm afraid so,' said Clara gently, but Ralph just rolled his eyes again, thinking Bing was being extraordinarily obtuse. Ralph tolerated fools marginally less than he tolerated first class service on a commercial jet.

Bing said, still in a state of partial befuddlement, 'But why have they kidnapped all of us? They only needed one of us to get the secret recipe.'

Clara said, with a mildly disapproving glance at the man seated next to her on the overstuffed pink sofa, 'Ralph thinks it's in case they can't torture the recipe out of any one of us, but I think he's being melodramatic.'

Strangely, the word torture made Bing think about his ferret Olivia. But probably only because she had the same name as his first wife. There was a frightening thought. They could use the medieval rack, the fingernail bamboos, even the Chinese Water Torture, and he would remain as silent as the Sphinx. But put him alone in a room with his first wife for a couple of hours and he would have given up the secret formula, the pin numbers of his cash cards and even the location of the Holy Grail if he'd known it.

'I think the truth is much less frightening, from a personal point of view,' Clara continued, 'but rather more terrifying for the company.'

Bing's beleaguered brain cells started functioning properly then, and he realised the answer even before she said it.

'They want the secret recipe all right,' she said. 'And they want to be the only ones who have it.'

Ralph harrumphed as if he still thought they were about to be tortured at any moment, but he conceded, 'Without the three of us, without the secret recipe, we'll be forced to use up all our reserve stock of the formula. That'll only last about two months, and after that,' he lowered his eyebrows and glowered at Bing as if it were all his fault, 'there won't be any Coca-Cola at all!'

A few thousand miles away, almost exactly the same words were being spoken by a swarthy, Mediterranean-looking gentleman named Ricardo Pansier.

HEAD OFFICE

In the corner of the boardroom stood a mechanical organ-grinder with a robotic monkey, and nobody knew what it symbolised, or what it was, or what it was doing there. But it had been there since forever, and nobody was brave enough to move it, in case it should turn out to be some incredibly ancient and valuable heirloom that had great significance to the company, The Coca-Cola Company.

The organ-grinder looked through glazed marble eyes at the heavily suited executives seated around the ornate polished walnut boardroom table in the ornate polished walnut boardroom of the company.

The robotic monkey wasn't interested in the executives. It just stared at the organ-grinder and held out a little tin cup as if expecting a coin or two.

None was forthcoming.

Ricardo Pansier, Vice-President (Production), actually pounded the polished walnut of the table with his fist, which was no way to treat polished walnut.

'Without the three of them,' he proclaimed, 'without the secret recipe, we'll be forced to use up all our reserve stock of the formula. That'll only last about two months, and after that,' he loosened his tie with a rigid finger and unbuttoned the expensive pinstriped collar of his expensive pinstriped shirt, 'there won't be any Coca-Cola at all!'

Ricardo was no panic merchant. You don't get to be VP (Production) for a company like The Coca-Cola Company if you are a panic merchant. So the loosened tie and the physical abuse of the quite innocent walnut table were probably about as close to panic as anyone had ever seen him.

The room was full of Vice-Presidents. Of course, no-one beneath that worthy rank would have made it past the ever-vigilant security guards stationed outside, cleverly disguised in collar, tie and rimless glasses, so that any one who entered the top floor of the Coca-Cola headquarters would think no more than, 'There are some security guards cleverly disguised as office workers.'

And on a day like today, only a fire, earthquake, or a fall in the stock price would have admitted anyone less than a Vice-President into that room. A disaster beyond the imagination of any of them was about to occur, and that was certainly not for the ears of the great unwashed.

There was no CEO, which was unusual. There was no Chairman of the Board, which was doubly unusual, and there was no Vice-Chairman, which was even more unusual, unless you considered that, at that moment, the three individuals just mentioned were sitting on an overstuffed pink sofa on a medium-sized private yacht somewhere in the Pacific Ocean. Which, just for the record, is a very big ocean.

Reginald Fairweather was a Vice-President, so he was at the meeting. And he had been a Vice-President a damn sight longer than Ricardo Pansier, who he considered to be a jumped-up upstart who had risen far too quickly through the ranks at The

Coca-Cola Company and now held a position he was in no way ready for. R.G. Fairweather, as the nameplate said on the table in front of him, had been a Vice-President for over twenty years, and was considered next in line for one of the big three positions should any of them, Heaven forbid, fall vacant.

Except that, Heaven's forbidding aside, all three positions seemed to be currently vacant and, in the eyes of most, that made R.G. Fairweather the man in charge.

'Ricky,' Reginald said, using the diminutive, although he would have glared at anyone who dared to call him 'Reggie'. 'Ricky, I don't want problems. I want a solution. What are we doing to resolve this issue?'

The way he said 'resolve this issue' made it sound as though he were worried about a faulty pipe in one of the factories, or an employee in need of major breath therapy, instead of a problem that could conceivably put The Coca-Cola Company out of business.

Borkin, VP (Security), cleared her throat. 'We know when and where each person was snatched. The FBI have the van from the Bahamas and the limousine from New Jersey. The Lear Jet has been cordoned off and we are awaiting a forensic team to reach it and start their analysis. But ...' She broke off a little uncertainly.

'Yes?' Reginald asked.

'If it is anything like the other two vehicles, we'll find nothing. Very professional job.'

'But the police are searching?'

'Police, FBI, Coastguard and Interpol are all active participants in the investigation,' Borkin said confidently. 'Plus I have two private detective firms following up some loose ends:

one in the Bahamas, and one in New Jersey. We'll turn up something.'

'You may turn up three bodies,' Ricardo intoned into a sudden silence.

Borkin shook her head. 'That's a possibility but, unless it's proven to be true, we act on the assumption that they are still alive. All of us.' She placed two hands firmly on the table top and stared at Ricardo. 'And we will find them.'

Reginald nodded. Borkin was efficient to the point of ruthlessness if she had to be. 'But will we be in time? Realistically, Ricky, how long have we got?'

Ricardo quietly ground his teeth every time he was referred to as 'Ricky', but Reginald had superiority, so he just smiled, put up with it and saw a very good dentist.

'Each bottling plant has stock on hand. We have the central reserves. I'd say we could still be supplying product for, say, three months. Maybe a few weeks more, but that would be the end of it.'

'Imagine that,' said Dolores Whitaker, the widow of former VP (Marketing) Delaney Whitaker, who had taken over his seat on the board. 'Imagine a world without Coca-Cola.'

'It's unthinkable,' snapped Keelan McCafferty, VP (Public Affairs). 'Coca-Cola is as American as Mom, God and apple pie! We can't let this happen.'

'Actually,' Borkin pointed out, 'I'm not sure that God is an American.'

But no-one listened as Keelan continued. 'Isn't there anyone else in the company who knows? Even half of it. Can't we work it out? Can't we guess?'

Ricardo said slowly, 'People have been guessing at it for years. Nobody has got it right yet. I don't see how we could expect to do any better. And, as far as I am aware, nobody else within the company actually knows. Reginald?'

Reginald nodded and shook his head at the same time, making a circular motion that confused everybody, including himself. 'I've been at the company for forty years, and I haven't got an inkling.'

'What about that scientist in Japan?' Dolores asked. 'He claims to have the recipe.'

Ricardo shook his head. 'I have one hundred and twenty three "recipes" sitting in a folder on my desk from people who claim to have worked it out. Maybe some of them have got it right. We could mix them up and see. *But how would we know?*'

'Remember New Coke?' Reginald said. 'We did hundreds of taste tests and millions of dollars of market research before changing our formula to one that most people preferred, and which they preferred to all our competitors' products. Yet it survived just a few months before public pressure forced us to change back to the original recipe. And that product was *advertised!* If we just pump out a new batch of Coke without telling anyone, and it's wrong, there'll be chaos. There'll be a lynching!'

There was much nodding around the table, and a black mood of despondency settled. Borkin's investigation was their only hope. But there was precious little time.

Terry Capper, VP (International), spoke up then. A small man with thick glasses who had hair growing out of his neck, tentacles of which crept out from his collar. He was intelligent, with three college degrees to prove it. He said, 'Actually there might be a way.'

He passed around photocopies of a memo he had just received from a small country in the South Pacific Ocean, which most of those present mistakenly thought was an island off the coast of Australia.

'There might just be a way,' he repeated, but they were all reading the memo, and nobody paid him any attention, except the mechanical organ-grinder in the corner.

FLEA'S PARTY

Flea's parents were away that weekend, so Flea organised a party.

It said a lot about Flea's parents that they were prepared to trust him, at just fifteen years old, to have a party while they were away, without trashing the whole house. But, perhaps, it actually said more about Flea. He was very mature for his age.

They had plenty to drink at the party. Three days after Fizzer and Tupai had been to see Coca-Cola Amatil in Mt Wellington, a courier van had turned up at Fizzer's home. The courier-guy had unloaded three large boxes, which had turned out to contain cans and cans and cans of Coke, along with Sprite, and quite a few cans of Fanta. Cases of them. There was a box of collectible Coca-Cola badges and a short note from Harry Truman too, which said simply, 'Thanks'.

It's a funny age to have a party, fifteen. You're too old for party games and kids' stuff like that. But you're a bit too self-conscious to dance. So they sat around and talked, and told rude jokes, except Tupai.

Tupai wasn't especially tall, and his shoulders were broad like the harbour bridge. But for all that, he could dance like Michael Jackson. Jenny was quite a dancer too, and it wasn't long before Tupai and Jenny were boogying away in the centre of the room to some band who'd just had a hit record.

A bunch of the girls who'd been invited were dancing too. There was Cherie, whose dad owned a brewery, a small boutique one in the city; Johanna and Christiana, exchange students from Switzerland who were identical twins and even blinked at the same time; Kelly, who bussed to school each day from Orewa, about an hour's ride, because her mum was a fan of international supermodel Rachel Hunter and wanted Kelly to go to the same school Rachel had been to. There was Lynne who wanted to be an opera singer, Annette who wanted to play representative hockey, and Erica, who Tupai had admired from a distance since the beginning of time. (About six months.) Erica was Scottish, blonde, with her hair cut short in a trendy shaggy style, and she had a delightful light burr of an accent. She had a fair complexion that looked at odds with the healthy tans the rest of them sported, and her eyelashes naturally curled around her eyes without any assistance from make-up or machinery. But she does not have any part to play in this story so that's enough about her.

She was lovely though.

The rest of them just kind of hung out and watched the dancers, especially Phil, who didn't take his eyes off Tupai and Jenny the entire time. Everyone agreed it was a great party, at least until the school seniors turned up with a keg of beer.

The party was for Fizzer, and everybody knew that, but nobody said anything about it. In the space of a few weeks Fizzer's world had been destroyed, then recreated. They were celebrating his spirit, his very essence, which had returned redoubled. But there was no way of saying that without sounding like a dork, so nobody said anything.

The party was at Flea's place because that was easily the best place for it. Jason had a rumpus room in his house but it was filled with cane and the frames of wicker chairs that his mum used in her hobby/craft business. Tupai's place was in a very rough part of town, and Fizzer lived with his dad in a caravan on the overgrown edge of a motor camp, down by an inlet of the upper harbour that was filled with mud and mangroves and smelled like a sewer when the tide was out. Not exactly party central.

There was a knock on the double glass ranch-sliders which led to the small courtyard and English cottage garden outside.

It was the first of their two unexpected visitors that evening (not counting the sixth formers with the keg of beer). A huge man, with a grin to match, impeccably dressed in dark trousers and a casual dress jacket, with a white t-shirt underneath.

'Henry!' Flea exclaimed, and they shook hands warmly, with two hands, the way guys do when they really want to hug each other but know it's not cool.

'Come in,' Flea said, after shaking hands for a very long time.

Henry had been Flea's best mate the year he had played rugby league professionally, and many said it was their combination of skills that had won the Premiership for their team.

'Hi, Jason, Tupai, Fizzer.'

Two years, and he still remembered their names.

'Hey, Henry!'

'How's the Spitfire?'

Fizzer laughed. Henry was talking about a secret playground they'd once shown him. A place called the Lost Park that the city council had forgotten existed.

'It's gone. The whole park is gone. I think the council must have found it on a map. They're building an apartment block there now.'

Henry laughed too, and Flea. None of them really knew why they laughed about it. It was one of the last vestiges of their childhood. Flattened under the bulldozers of city developers. It wasn't really funny; it was a tragedy. Maybe that's why they laughed.

Henry grabbed a Coke and settled into a corner with Flea for a bit of a catch up. A few of the others sat in a circle around them, awed by the presence of such a big rugby league star, although, when you thought about it, he was no more famous than Flea.

Phil had brought his drums. As a drummer he was a good singer. As a singer, he probably would be better off playing guitar. And he couldn't play guitar at all. He wanted to form a band, and wanted Fizzer (harmonica) and Tupai (guitar) to be in it, along with James McDonald (bass guitar), brother of the lovely, Scottish object of Tupai's unrequited affection: Erica McDonald.

Both Tupai and Fizzer had been trying to avoid getting involved in a band with Phil, but he had talked them into having a few practices together.

Phil went out to get his drums from the car, but when he came back carrying his snares, he had unwanted company: a bunch of yahoos from the senior school, who always seemed to turn up at parties and then invite their friends over. One time at Hamish Knox's place so many had turned up, using their mobile phones to text their friends, who then turned up and texted *their* friends, that it turned into a near riot and the police had to be called, with the Eagle police helicopter and their riot helmets, long batons and other assorted equipment for the purpose of dispersing rioters.

There were two car loads this night, but Flea saw them coming and met them at the door. Tupai had also seen them, and he was right alongside Flea when they arrived.

Henry looked up with interest, but no obvious concern. Most of the dancers were still dancing, and the party was still going on all around them.

Flea was firm. 'Sorry, guys, invitation only.'

One of them made a disparaging remark, and the others laughed.

Tupai said, 'Another night, eh?'

They were a bit wary of Tupai. His reputation had grown with the number of fights that he'd got into, and the number of bloodied noses and black eyes he'd left in his wake. The 'strongest kid in school' reputation that had seemed like so much fun at primary school had turned into 'the toughest kid in school' reputation at secondary school, and all the other kids, including seniors, who thought they deserved to hold that title, were always lining up to have a go at Tupai.

Big mistake. Tupai had never lost a fight in his life. At the age of fourteen, he had been attacked by two seventh formers *at the same time* and had left them bloodied and crying.

But there were at least eight of the gatecrashers hanging around outside the ranch-sliders, standing on plants, generally making a right nuisance of themselves and trying to get inside.

Fizzer and Jason joined their friends at the door.

'Look out, your mum's arrived,' the closest one sneered, who seemed to be some kind of ring-leader. 'And your girlfriend too. What beautiful hair.'

Fizzer was growing his hair long and had it tied back in a short ponytail.

Tupai visibly bristled at the slur but said calmly, 'You don't want to gatecrash this party, guys.'

'Actually, we do. That's why we're standing in this stupid, ugly garden waiting for you to get out of the way.'

The guy's name was Carl. He was large and podgy with horrible acne. Even his mates called him 'crater-face' behind his back, and to those in the junior school he was known as 'the thing from the swamp'.

His attitude seemed to match his acne.

Tupai never lost his cool, not for one second. He said, 'This is a junior school party. It's just a bunch of kids sitting around drinking soft drinks and playing party games. You don't want to come in here, you'll never live it down.'

There was a murmuring from crater-face's mates.

Tupai resumed his softly spoken speech. 'I heard there was a party at Mike Shanaghan's tonight. That's where all the cool people are.'

That was all it took. There was a short, muttered conference amongst the hydrangeas and fuchsias, then they were gone. Not even a backward glance or departing repartee. The kid who had never lost a fight was learning how to avoid them.

As if he had been waiting for them to leave, a tall, slim man stepped into the pool of light in the courtyard as the seniors drifted away, trampling across the lawn. He had broad shoulders like a swimmer. He smiled warmly at Tupai then his eyes settled on Fizzer.

'Hi, Fraser,' he said. 'I rang your place, your dad told me where you were.'

Tupai seemed stunned to see the man. Fizzer seemed, almost (just almost), not to be surprised.

'Hi, Mr Truman,' Fizzer said. 'Guys, this is Harry Truman, from Coca-Cola.'

They all stepped outside then, as the music was too loud in the room for easy conversation.

'I'm sorry to interrupt your party,' Harry said, 'but a very tricky problem has developed at our head office in Atlanta.' He paused and looked seriously at Fizzer. 'Do you have a passport?'

Fizzer shook his head.

Later that evening, against all odds, Erica McDonald asked Tupai to dance.

ATLANTA

Anastasia Borkin was a Russian. Not from one of the satellite states of the former USSR, who were often mistakenly called Russians, but from Mother Russia herself. She looked like a Russian too, in that broad-jawed Slavic way. But her long, softly curling, brown hair, and the artful use of make-up softened that appearance, and her twinkling, sparkling smile lit up her face like a fireworks display, and was worth a fortune in cosmetic surgery. Most of the men she had known throughout her life had thought her quite attractive, in a broad-jawed Slavic sort of way.

Anastasia Borkin was Vice-President (Security) for The Coca-Cola Company. That a Russian should hold such a post as Vice-President (Security) for a bastion of Americanism like The Coca-Cola Company seemed like a strange international irony, but really it was no more than a person who happened to be particularly good at her job rising, through talent and hard work, to a position of high authority.

And in any case, anyone who knew their history would know that a Russian named after the long-lost daughter of the last of the Russian Tsars would be no great comrade of the communist government in that country.

Born in New York, the daughter of a Russian defector, she sometimes wondered if her father had really been a spy, but there was no evidence and her father emphatically denied it right up until his death.

Borkin was Russia mad. She studied Russian music and poetry and collected paintings by great Russian painters. She helped fund a small cinema that ran Russian films. She was a keen chess player and avidly studied the great Russian chess masters. She was a fan of Russia the same way some people are fans of baseball, or certain breeds of dog. Not that she would ever want to live there. The thought of giving up a comfortable life in a warm southern state for bleak winters in Moscow was not even an option for discussion, and her young family would have absolutely mutinied.

Anastasia Borkin was a Russian. That's what she told everyone. But scratch the hide of the Russian bear and the Stars and Stripes shone through.

Borkin smiled as the two New Zealand boys emerged apprehensively out of the customs area of Hartsfield International Airport. A flight attendant walked alongside, chatting animatedly with them. Their flight chaperone no doubt. The board had insisted on an airline chaperone, and also insisted one of the Vice-Presidents meet them at the airport. As VP (Security) Borkin had felt it was her responsibility and, as much as she disliked the idea of babysitting, seeing them gave her a small hope that it might not be quite as arduous a duty as she had feared.

Borkin stepped forward as the three approached, the boys looking around uncertainly. 'Mr Boyd and Mr White?' she asked.

The taller one stuck out a hand in greeting and said warmly, 'G'day. I'm Fraser.'

'Gidday,' Borkin said, a little awkwardly, trying to make the lad feel at home.

'Tupai,' said the other, with a smile as wide as Gorky Park.

'I'm Anastasia Borkin,' she said. 'I'm a Vice-President with Coca-Cola. I'll escort you to our offices.' She turned to the chaperone, smart and sharp in her Qantas uniform, and said, 'Everything go all right on the flight?'

'Oh, they weren't any trouble at all,' the chaperone said, and gave Borkin a knowing wink that made her wonder just what she was in for.

'See ya later, Jan,' Fraser said.

'See ya,' Tupai echoed.

To Anastasia's surprise the flight attendant, Jan, impulsively reached out and hugged each of the boys in turn. 'You be good,' she said.

The two boys hugged her back, without embarrassment or backslapping, but with real affection.

Borkin's broad Slavic jaw wrinkled into a half smile. They must have made quite an impression on their chaperone, she thought. She was still smiling as they made their way out of the terminal to where their driver was waiting.

The boys were fascinated by the limousine. Bright red, with white suede upholstery. Coca-Cola colours of course. Tupai opened a small fridge in the centre of the limo and, for some reason, seemed surprised to find it stocked, not with champagne, but with Coca-Cola. Having opened the fridge, however, he was having some trouble getting it closed. It popped up out of an island in the centre of the limo and created a small table as it did so. But it wouldn't pop back down. He pressed it down, but each time it just sprang back up. Eventually Borkin, with a polite smile, reached across and shut it for him. Fraser just stared out of the window, seemingly overwhelmed by the sheer scale of all things American.

'I heard you had to get a passport in quite a hurry,' Borkin said.

Fraser nodded. 'Never been overseas before. Never even been on a plane before.' He pulled his passport out of a pocket in his jeans and showed it to her proudly.

'Never been on a plane?' Borkin was a little surprised. She knew very little about New Zealand, but surely they had planes.

Fraser continued. 'Nope. And I don't think the assistant had used the camera before. Look, I look like an escapee from a home for the weird.'

Tupai laughed. 'You are an escapee from a home for the weird.'

Borkin laughed with him. 'How about you, Tupai, did you have a passport?'

'Yeah, I got one when I went wallaby hunting in Oz with my old man.'

Borkin looked blankly at him for a moment, and eventually asked, 'You like hunting?'

'Crikey, yeah!' Fraser exclaimed. 'Tupai and his dad get themselves dropped off by helicopter in the middle of the bush, two weeks from the nearest civilisation, with just two days' supply of food. They live off the land on the way out.' There was a grudging admiration in his voice, but it was clear from his expression that he felt it was something you'd be sentenced to if you'd committed a major crime, rather than something you did for fun.

'It's great,' Tupai smiled. 'The only bit I'm not too keen on is burning off the leeches after a trek through a swamp.'

Fraser shuddered comically.

'Are there wild animals in New Zealand?' Borkin asked.

'Well, there're the Captain Cookers,' Tupai replied.

'Captain Cookers?'

'Huge wild pigs,' Fraser explained. 'Big tusks, charge right at you.'

'But they're all right.' Tupai grinned. 'It's the moas you've got to worry about. Giant birds, three metres tall. Legs like small trees. Sharp claws.'

'Holy Cow,' Borkin whispered, wondering what kind of a place they came from.

Fraser and Tupai looked at each other, then both burst into laughter. At some point, Borkin realised, they had started teasing her. Only she wasn't quite sure where that point was.

Anastasia Borkin decided she was going to enjoy the company of these two exuberant young men.

COCA-COLA PLAZA

Tupai had come on the journey because Fizzer, who considered himself generally to be at one with the universe, had never been at one with any part of the universe other than New Zealand, and the thought of wandering around a foreign country without at least one friendly face was a little daunting, even for Fizzer, imperturbable Fizzer.

Fizzer had asked Harry if Tupai could go, and Harry had approved it without even consulting his superiors in Atlanta, which had made them realise that, whatever was going on, it was pretty *big stuff*!

Not two days after his passport arrived – in a plain brown envelope at the office of the motor camp – Fizzer and Tupai pulled up outside Coca-Cola headquarters in a bright red limousine with Anastasia Borkin.

Coca-Cola headquarters turned out to be not one building but four. It was situated on a road named after the company, Coca-Cola Plaza, stuck right in the middle of North Avenue, Downtown, Atlanta, Georgia, on the south-eastern side of the United States of America.

A massive Coca-Cola symbol stared down at them from the tallest of the buildings as they were ushered, like VIPs, up the steps of the smallest building, which turned out to be the corporate headquarters.

There was some compulsory handshaking with a bunch of Important People, with names that both of them forgot as soon as they heard them, overawed, as they were, by the whole process. Then they were whisked off to the tallest of the buildings, in through a huge reception area with floor to ceiling windows and shiny black floors. The windows were covered with a colourful tapestry of transparencies: photographs of Coca-Cola employees and their personal stories.

They passed through corridors where Coke was dispensed in cans from free vending machines or flowed from soda fountains, up in a plushly upholstered lift, or 'elevator' as their hosts called it, and eventually into a large room panelled in a dark, rich wood with a matching table that stretched the length of the room.

Here, there were more introductions: Mr Fairweather was a tall, grey-haired man with an angular Adam's apple that bobbed as he spoke; Mr Pansier looked Italian, but spoke with a slow Texan drawl; Mr Capper looked for all the world like a kiwifruit, with little brown hairs sprouting in all directions; Mr McCafferty was young and friendly, but there was a fierce determination behind his eyes; Mrs Whitaker was a rather severe-looking lady in her fifties.

A series of ten plastic tumblers were set up on small white paper coasters in a row along one side of the table.

The tall man, Mr Fairweather, indicated to Tupai and Fizzer that they should sit down in front of the tumblers, but it was Mr Pansier who spoke.

'Reports are that you have quite a discerning palate when it comes to soft drinks.'

Fizzer nodded. It seemed easier than talking in front of all these important-looking executives in their dark suits.

'Naturally we are a little sceptical,' Mr Pansier continued, 'but if it turns out to be true, then your talents could possibly have a small practical application in some new field trials that we are planning.'

Tupai and Fizzer looked at each other. They may have been young, naïve and from a small country at the bottom of the world, but neither was foolish enough to believe that they had been whisked away from New Zealand at a moment's notice and were now standing in front of a bunch of high-powered executives just because Fizzer might be able to assist with a field trial.

Mr Pansier's manner was friendly, but there was a small bite of disbelief in his voice. 'If what is claimed about you is true, then you'll be able to pass this simple test we have prepared for you.'

He indicated the tumblers.

'All of these glasses contain cola drinks. One of them contains our own product, Coca-Cola. We'd like you to see if you can identify it.'

They're not glasses, Fizzer thought, they're plastic tumblers, but he nodded anyway.

'Take your time,' Mr Pansier said, meaning that Fizzer should start.

'Could I have a glass of water?' Fizzer asked. 'And a bucket? Oh, and a pen and some paper.'

There was a small delay while these were fetched, during which Fizzer noticed a small, discrete smile trickle out from the face of Anastasia, just a few sparklers, not the full fireworks display, as if she had suggested this herself earlier but had been overruled.

Tupai folded his arms and tried to look like a bouncer because he was a bit nervous and had nothing much else to do.

When the water arrived, Fizzer took a sip, rinsed it around inside his mouth, then spat it into the bucket. It seemed a crass thing to do in front of high-powered executives in such a posh boardroom, and he caught a disapproving glance from Mr Pansier, but Anastasia winked at him and he relaxed and smiled back at her.

Fizzer went quickly down the line of drinks, watching the bubbles, sniffing the tumblers, sampling the drinks, rinsing his mouth between each one, pretty much the same routine as at the Glenfield school fair. The main difference was the notes that he jotted down on the supplied notepad as he went. He finished the last sample, rinsed his mouth for a final time, and sat down studying his notes.

'Any luck?' Mrs Whitaker asked gently.

There was a silence, during which even Tupai began to look doubtful.

Mr Pansier crossed his arms and leaned back in his chair, shaking his head sceptically.

Eventually Fizzer looked up. He said quietly, 'These drinks have been sitting here too long. You should have waited for me to arrive before you poured them.'

Mr Pansier started to say something but stopped as Fizzer continued firmly, 'Also, you served them in plastic tumblers. You should have used paper. You can taste the plastic. However …'

He looked around the table, then back down at his notes.

'You have also lied to me, saying that only one of these drinks was Coca-Cola.'

Mr Pansier looked indignant, but caught a menacing glare from Tupai, whose menacing glares would frighten a wild animal, and said nothing.

Fizzer continued. 'They're all Coca-Cola, except for the last one which is Diet-Coke. The first three are out of a can, the first two of which were poured quickly, but the third one was left to sit in the can for a while before it was poured. Number four is from a small plastic bottle, about a half litre bottle, I'm not sure if you use the same sized bottles here as we do in New Zealand. Number five is from the same sized bottle, but *not the same bottle*, as number four. Six, seven and eight are from a larger bottle, at least two litres, and number nine is from a post-mix dispenser like a soda fountain.'

There was general surprise around the table, and Mr Pansier in particular looked absolutely flabbergasted, but Fizzer hadn't finished.

'I wouldn't stake my life on any of this, however, because the drinks all taste a little strange to me. I suspect you might use a different sweetener here in the States than we do back home. Maybe corn syrup instead of cane sugar. Something like that, I can't be sure.'

He put his notes down and looked a little guiltily around the room. 'Sorry.'

Mr Fairweather looked at Mr Pansier. 'Well, Ricky, how did the lad do?'

Mr Pansier looked stunned. As a pretext for delay, he opened a folder in front of him and pretended to scan a few sheets.

Eventually, just when the wait was getting embarrassing, he said, 'I think he's right, pretty much, although it was a sixteen-ounce bottle, numbers four and five.'

'Fraser did say *about half a litre,*' Anastasia reminded him. 'And half a litre is five hundred mil, which is near as dammit to a sixteen-ounce bottle.'

Mr McCafferty was more direct. 'Let me get this straight. This kid can tell the difference between the taste of Coke from a big bottle, and Coke from a small bottle, and you're quibbling over a few mil! Hell,' he tossed his pen down on the table in amazement, 'I couldn't tell Coke in a can from Coke in a bottle, and I work for the company! What kind of a test was this anyway?'

'I … er,' Mr Pansier started, but Mr Fairweather held up a hand and cut him off.

'He was right about the sweetener too. So does anyone have any doubts about Fraser's ability to help us out of our little … difficulty?'

There was a unanimous shaking of heads.

'OK, Fraser,' he said, 'let's talk money.'

It turned out to be just as well that Tupai was there, as Fizzer, never having had much money, had no real idea how to negotiate financially. Also, he believed that if you did good in this world, then good came back to you through unexpected ways, so he would have done it for nothing if it came to that. Karma he called it, (although, actually, Karma is a much more complicated concept than that).

Tupai, on the other hand, found the negotiation process a little like a street fight and jumped in boots and all. Helped, no doubt, by the fact that, unknown to him, the people at that table were desperate enough to have mortgaged the company if they'd had to.

The actual amount they arrived at is highly confidential, and there are several severe penalties for revealing it. But suffice to say that Fizzer and his dad would no longer be living in a caravan park by a smelly mangrove swamp, and Fizzer would not have to pay his way through university. He could also have purchased a brand new convertible Italian sports car if he'd wanted to, but he didn't have a driver's licence and, anyway, he wasn't into that sort of ostentatious display of wealth. Money had very little meaning for Fizzer.

Tupai also accepted a modest fee, for no other reason than that they offered it. There was even the prospect of a job at Coca-Cola for Fizzer, after he had finished university, but that was too far ahead in the future to think about.

So Fizzer was appointed as a Coca-Cola taster on a short-term contract, and Tupai was appointed as his assistant.

Fizzer possessed good, almost uncanny intuition. But he was not psychic; he could not see the future. And that's a real shame, because, if he had known what was in store for him, he might have turned the job down.

THE SECRET RECIPE

The lock on the far doors of the yacht's lounge snicked loudly, and the twin handles began to turn.

A man and a woman entered. He was holding a menacing-looking pistol in his right hand, while she carried a clump of small, spiral-bound notepads and a handful of pens. In truth, any pistol looks menacing when it is pointed at you, and this one was pointed unfalteringly at the three of them seated on the pink couch.

Clara Fogsworth's first thought on seeing the weapon was, 'How rude,' for it is certainly not the height of decorum to aim a gun at another person, especially an elderly, unarmed person. But then she looked at the man's face, and she was no longer surprised.

Ralph Winkler just grunted, as if he had been expecting this all along, and the sooner they got it over with the better. He did think, though, that he might have seen the gentleman with the gun somewhere before, but he couldn't quite remember where.

Bingham Statham sat with his lower jaw touching his chest in total shock at this latest turn of events. He didn't know the man with the gun from a bar of lavender-scented soap, but he recognised the woman all right.

'Hello, Bingo,' she said, using her private name for him that he'd always thought was a bit silly. 'It's a real pleasure to see you again, considering the circumstances.'

'Hello, Candy,' Bing said, thinking maybe he should have mounted her head on his trophy wall while he'd had the chance.

Clara still said nothing. She was quite determined not to, in fact. The absolute curmudgeon! Tall, handsome and athletic he might be, but Mr Joseph Sturdee was nothing more than an amoeba on the scale of worldwide evolution as far as she was concerned.

Then Ralph finally clicked. 'You're that actor,' he blurted out, as if it were a crime in itself. 'You play Doctor Messenger on *The Beautiful Years.*'

Joseph Sturdee's smile was as menacing as the gun. 'Used to play.' He had given that smile daily, terrorising the other characters in the soap opera for over fifteen years, just to be dumped, unwanted by the network, booed and pelted in the street by fans. All because he had left his real-life wife, the popular and charismatic Pepper Green, to have an affair with Candy Statham, the wife of the Coke millionaire.

And to top it all off, Pepper had sued him and won millions! Not that she needed the money. Her star shot up like a comet after the affair, and her character on the programme became one of its hottest properties.

All Bing could think of to say to Candy was, 'I had a ferret named after you. It died.'

'How sweet, how very touching in fact, but now that we've exchanged pleasantries, we have a little business to attend to.' Brusque and business-like, Candy bustled around the room, handing out pads and pens, while ushering Ralph and Bing to seats on opposite sides of the cabin.

While all this was happening, Bing thought that Candy was quite wrong. About the ferret. It was neither sweet nor touching. He'd read somewhere that those who cannot remember the past are condemned to repeat it. And so he'd named his ferrets after his two ex-wives, to remind him of his mistakes.

'I want you each to write out the formula for Coca-Cola,' Candy said brightly. She'd had another face-lift since he'd last seen her, and the skin was drawn tautly across her cheekbones, giving her a pastiche semblance of youth.

'When you've finished, hand it to me. I'm going to compare each of your recipes with each of the others. If yours doesn't agree, then Joe here is going to throw you over the side.'

'And we're a long, long way from land,' Joe added, rather unnecessarily.

'I'm quite sure that as soon as we've finished writing, you're going to tip us over the side anyway,' said Ralph gloomily. 'You won't need us any more.'

Clara and Bing glanced across at each other, the same thought on their minds.

'Oh, don't be so silly,' Candy said. 'We're kidnappers not murderers. No, we have a nice little retirement home planned for you where you can all live out the rest of your lives quietly, teaching each other to sing in peace and harmony.'

Nobody smiled at her oh-so-witty reference to the famous Coke ad of the seventies.

'Well, get writing!' she said testily.

HUBBLE, BUBBLE, TOIL AND TROUBLE

The first recipe they tried was the one from the scientist in Okinawa. Okinawa is a small island off the coast of Japan where Fizzer's school of karate originated, but that's just one of life's small coincidences and has absolutely nothing to do with this story.

Fizzer took one sip and spat it into the bucket. 'Are you sure you followed the recipe?'

Ricardo Pansier, who had changed his attitude considerably since the taste test in the boardroom, was sampling the brew also, and he screwed his face up but swallowed the mouthful.

'To the millilitre. And we've mixed up a few variations as well, just for comparison. Increased this a little, decreased that a little. They're all numbered.'

Rows of small plastic bottles, sealed, with numbers marked on them in black felt pen, covered the tray of a metal lab trolley that had been wheeled in a few moments earlier.

'Don't bother,' Fizzer said, a little unkindly, considering how much trouble they had gone to. 'It tastes more like soy sauce than it does like Coca-Cola.'

'What if we added more sugar?'

'Then it would taste like sweet soy sauce.'

'Oh.'

It turned out that Ricardo had a whole stack of recipes from all sorts of people who claimed to have deciphered the mystery of the secret recipe. Some were from crackpots, like the one from an old guy in Peru, who claimed he had been given the recipe by the ancient sun gods. His recipe included hair oil and alpaca turd, so was quickly discarded.

Other recipes had all manner of other ingredients in them, but because The Coca-Cola Company did not actually order that particular ingredient from anyone, over thirty of them could be rejected. A surprising number of them mistakenly included old tea leaves as a key ingredient.

The story about field trials had long been discarded, and Tupai and Fizzer had joined a small group of people who knew what was wrong within The Coca-Cola Company: the missing executives, who had come to be known as the 'Coca-Cola Three'; the production deadline; the terrible possibility that the formula for Coca-Cola might be gone forever!

One of the things that most surprised Tupai was how little the staff of the company actually knew about the recipe of their main product, and he asked how this was achieved.

'Come with me,' Ricardo said, as the next trolley was brought in.

They left Fizzer wincing with disgust at the contents of the first bottle and took an elevator, as Tupai was getting used to calling them, to the basement of the building. The elevator doors opened on a brightly lit corridor, white walls washed with banks of fluorescent tubes recessed into the ceiling.

The corridor led to a set of huge stainless steel doors watched over by three gargoyles, actually very polite young men in crisp black uniforms, with badges and hats that made them look like the policemen they weren't. Ricardo's authority was enough to gain entry for both of them, and they stepped inside a highly computerised control room.

You would be forgiven for imagining big banks of machines with flashing lights and spinning discs, but this was nothing like that. There were just seven computer monitors, no different from your home PC, with ordinary keyboards sitting in front of them.

There were three on the left of the control room, three on the right, all occupied by busy looking people with earnest expressions and too many pens in their top pockets. The other keyboard and monitor was unattended and by itself on a table in the centre of the room.

Ricardo gestured for Tupai to sit in the high-backed leather office chair that faced the empty monitor, and perched himself on the side of the desk.

He swept his hand around the room. 'You're in Coca-Cola Central. From here we monitor the huge vats that mix and boil the ingredients in various combinations to get the final syrup. There are factories in Africa, Ireland and Puerto Rico, all linked up to this central command station right here.'

Tupai glanced around. One petite Asian lady in a white coat gave him a small smile, but the others concentrated on their screens.

Ricardo said, 'I am the Vice-President in charge of Production here at Coca-Cola, which means that I know more about what happens in those vats than anyone else in the company, and yet I still have no idea what's in the formula.'

He pointed to the screen, and Tupai saw a list of ingredients, each with a blank field beside it. 'Isn't this your list of ingredients?' he asked. 'Surely with this list you're halfway home!'

Ricardo sighed. 'I wish it were that simple. We buy a lot of ingredients. I'm not even sure that we use all of them; some might be purchased simply to throw our competitors off the scent. The actual percentages of the ingredients are entered here, by one of the Coca-Cola Three. They have to do that at the end of each mixing cycle, about once a week. All waste, including any unused ingredients, is incinerated, so there's no way of knowing what is or isn't used.' He tapped his finger on the screen, leaving a print. 'Look here. Lime Juice. Vanilla. Do we actually put lime juice in Coca-Cola? I don't know. Maybe they enter zero in that field and all the lime juice goes to the incinerator. But even if we knew the exact ingredients, and the exact percentages, we'd still only be halfway there. The next stage of the process is combining them all. I know that some of the ingredients get mixed together, boiled, and cooled before being added to the other ingredients. But I don't know which ones. That's the job of the recipe holders. They program it all in here as well.

Right now we're at the end of the mixing cycle. The computer is sitting here waiting for the numbers to be entered.'

'What if they stuffed it up?' Tupai asked, and seeing the blank look, rephrased himself. 'Got the numbers wrong.'

Ricardo nodded as if it had been an intelligent question. 'It takes two of them, you know. One enters the data, then another one comes in and re-enters the same data. If the numbers don't match perfectly, the machines won't run.'

Tupai pursed his lips. 'Smart system.'

Ricardo laughed bitterly. 'Maybe too smart for our own good.'

'Why isn't the recipe written down somewhere, for safekeeping, for an emergency such as this?' Tupai asked.

'It used to be. It was held in the company safe. But there was a court case in '96, part of a divorce proceedings, arguing over the ownership of a written recipe that may or may not have been old John Pemberton's, that's the guy who invented Coke, his original notes. I think then the board realised that if it was written down on paper, it was bound to show up somewhere before too long, or get published on the Internet. So all written copies were destroyed. Now it's only held in the brains of a few selected employees. Never fewer than three of them.'

Tupai looked up at the dark eyes of the Vice-President (Production). They were filled with a passion, a pride in the company and the product that was famous throughout the world. Here in the control room, the central nervous system of a creature that reached tentacles out into the furthest corners of the globe, he could begin to feel the same excitement. Over a hundred years of history and an enterprise so colossal it beggared imagination.

And in feeling the passion, for the first time, he felt the fear. The fear that it could soon all be over.

'How long have we got?' he asked, surprising himself by using the word 'we'.

'If we don't get these vats churning in about eight weeks,' Ricardo said quietly, 'a can of Coke is going to become a collector's item.'

When they arrived back, Fizzer was reading a football magazine and idly blowing a few tuneless, discordant notes on his harmonica. He looked bored.

'We've been through three batches,' he said. 'Apparently that's all they can do today.'

Ricardo nodded. 'They'll have to clean and sterilise all the equipment now. Start preparing the next batches. They'll work on it through the night, taking it in shifts. We'll have another try in the morning. I'll call a car to take you to your hotel.'

Staying in a flash hotel seemed like a pretty cool thing to both Fizzer and Tupai, neither of whom had ever done it, but they both managed to act quite nonchalant, as if it were an everyday occurrence for them.

'The car will pick you up again tomorrow morning at seven, so we can get an early start on the tastings,' Ricardo said.

'What about dinner?' asked Tupai, despite the fact that he had eaten a full meal on the plane just a few hours ago, and, thanks to the different time zones, it was actually getting closer to breakfast time than dinner.

'Room service is great at the hotel. And you've got a huge TV in your room.'

'Cool!' Tupai said.

'How many channels?' Fizzer asked.

'Oh, I don't know. Fifty or so, I guess.'

'Cool!' Tupai said.

Ricardo said, 'So just relax. It's all paid for. Unless you'd like to have dinner with the board tonight?'

'Actually,' said Fizzer, 'I'd just like to get some sleep.'

733-23-A

The next day was much the same as the previous, as far as the tastings were concerned. Fizzer eliminated three batches in the morning, and they both received a personally guided tour of the Coca-Cola World interactive museum, by no less than Reginald Fairweather, while the scientists mixed up the afternoon's batches.

One of the afternoon mixes showed some promise, and there was considerable excitement when Fizzer suggested a few alterations that might help bring it closer to the actual recipe itself. But it turned out to be a bit of a red herring as, no matter how they played around with the recipe, it just kept getting further and further away.

The first week went by, and spirits never flagged. Each new recipe was brewed with the wide-eyed enthusiasm that this might just be the one. Each variation that Fizzer asked for was seized upon with a religious fervour, as though it might prove to be the holy grail of cola making.

But the week ended up as a lot of activity for absolutely no gain.

The second week was much the same, and the third week. The main difference on the fourth week was that the buoyant mood of hope and expectation, that Fizzer was the solution to all their woes, was starting to disappear.

The mood wasn't helped by the fact that the investigations into the disappearance of the three executives had gone precisely nowhere. There had been no clues left behind, no carelessly dropped book of matches with a phone number conveniently written inside. No cigarette butts of a foreign kind sold in certain shops by store owners with photographic memories for their customers.

Life wasn't like the movies, it seemed, and the location of the executives was proving as elusive as the secret formula itself.

Fizzer was beside himself on the Wednesday of the fifth week, jumping around the room, knocking things over. '483,' he kept shouting. 'Number 483.'

483 was the batch number of the bottle he had just tried. Fizzer could hardly contain himself, but Tupai wondered why the others were all so unexcited by the discovery.

It turned out that 483 was in fact Coca-Cola. Ricardo had sent a bottle filled with the real thing along amidst a bunch of other batches, just to make sure that Fizzer would actually know the stuff if he fell over it.

As a test of Fizzer's ability it was a success. But it got them no closer to finding the recipe, and when Fizzer finally realised the reason for all the glum faces, he was so depressed they took the rest of the afternoon off.

It was the last batch on the Friday of the sixth week that finally started unravelling the mystery.

Fizzer handed a capful of the dark liquid to Tupai to try. He did that occasionally, perhaps to keep Tupai involved in what was going on, although he said it was so that Tupai could educate his tastebuds.

'It's just a matter of perception and focus,' he'd said on more than one occasion.

Tupai washed the liquid around in his mouth, then swallowed it.

'What do you think?' Fizzer asked.

'Not quite,' Tupai said, 'but not too far away.'

'I've got a feeling about this one,' Fizzer said. 'It tastes right. Well, not right, exactly, but it tastes as though all the ingredients are there, just not quite in the right amounts.'

He scribbled some notes. Batch 733 it was. Three was his lucky number, but that had nothing to do with his feelings about the brew.

The next day, Saturday, they didn't have to work, and they'd been given some tickets to a football game, but Fizzer wanted to go in anyway. They'd have tried some of his suggestions on 733 by then.

733-23-A got Fizzer quite excited. He knew it wasn't another of Ricardo's tests because it had been mixed according to Fizzer's explicit instructions.

Tupai called Ricardo on his mobile and they were quite surprised when not just Ricardo, but Reginald, Keelan, Terry, and Dolores turned up in the lounge, along with Anastasia Borkin. News of the possible discovery was too big to hold in.

Fizzer explained a little about 733-23-A. 'But I'm not sure,' he said.

A few of the Vice-Presidents tried it and there was general concurrence that it was on the right track. The mood, which had been growing steadily darker over the past few weeks, lifted

72

like a blanket, and there were smiles and even a little laughter amongst the stressed out VPs.

Fizzer made some more notes for the next batch, then they left for the day. Tupai was quite keen to get to the Georgia Dome, where the home football team, the Atlanta Falcons, was playing that afternoon. They had only ever seen American Football on TV before, and Anastasia had generously bought them the tickets, so it was an opportunity not to be missed.

The limo that arrived was black, not the bright red one they were used to, which was the first warning sign they both completely missed.

The partition between the passenger compartment and the driver's seat was up, which was also unusual as they had got to know all the limo drivers by first name over the last six weeks and generally had a good chat on the way to where they were going.

If they hadn't been overexcited about batch 733-23-A, and maybe a little about the football game, they might have wondered why the fridge was already open, and why two long, cold glasses of water were waiting for them on the small table.

But they didn't.

After all the sticky sweet batches of cola, a cold glass of water was a blessed relief for both of them.

Fizzer looked quite tired, Tupai thought, a few minutes into their drive. In fact he looked as if he were out cold, lying back against the seat with his eyes shut and the glass about to slip out of his hand.

It had been a long, tiring six weeks after all, Tupai thought, and stretched out to take the glass from his friend's hand.

That's when the first wave of dizziness hit him, and his own glass dropped to the floor, soaking the plush carpet of the vehicle.

He tried to suck in some deep breaths to fight off an approaching cloud of haziness and nausea, but it didn't help, and by the time the limo had sped right past the queues waiting to get into the Georgia Dome, Tupai was stretched out on the seat of the car, snoring like a Captain Cooker.

HOLIDAY HOME FOR A TROLL

Clara Fogsworth had been underground before. She led quite an adventurous life and, although some of the more physical activities were becoming a little beyond her ageing bones, even as recently as a few years ago she had enjoyed some dare-devil adventures like waterskiing, jet boating and blackwater rafting. Her grandchildren thought it was really cool that she did these things, and called her Super Nana. Her children, two strong boys named Kurt and Stephan (she still called them boys even though they were in their forties) thought she was utterly mad, and their ever-so-pretty wives just smiled politely and rolled their eyes behind her back whenever she came to visit, and never came to visit her.

But no-one ever told her to give up the dangerous pursuits; in fact she suspected that at least one of the wives encouraged them.

Maybe it was due to the fact that they stood to inherit the millions of dollars of Coca-Cola shares that she and her late husband had amassed, ever since the 1940s, when it had seemed like part of the war effort to help build Coke factories overseas for the troops.

Oddly enough, if Clara's husband hadn't died of a tiny, but deadly, virus easily treated with modern medicine but often fatal back in the 1950s, she might never have taken up hang-gliding, or parachuting, or been in the space-flight simulator at the Kennedy Space Centre in Florida. 'You never know how long you've got,' she used to say to anyone who would listen. 'So you might as well live it while you've got it.'

Now in her late seventies, Clara knew she probably wasn't going to have it for all that much longer. A couple of decades at most, the last years of which she might be as helpless as a newborn baby.

None of which particularly concerned her, as she felt she had led a long, interesting and fruitful life, and would eventually go to her peace in the knowledge of a job well done. She just didn't want to spend those last couple of decades living in a hole in the ground. And the way she was going, that looked like a distinct possibility.

The way she was going was down. The helicopter that had brought them to the island was perched at the top of the sinkhole, a long cable attached to its winch slowly lowering her the thirty or so metres to the floor of the cave on which Bingham, dear, kind, easily befuddled Bingham, and Ralph, surly, glowering Ralph, waited for her.

The harness slithered back up the shaft the second she unbuckled it, and she looked around at her new home.

The floor of the cave was dry and sandy, and a small stream ran through the centre of it, disappearing into a hole in the rock at the lower end.

There were six smaller caves off the main cave, and one of those led to another smaller chamber beyond, but it seemed that the only way *out*, was *up*.

Three of the caves had been set up as bedrooms, with

stretcher beds, and drapes that could be hooked up to cover the entrances.

There was a small kerosene-powered refrigerator, and a seemingly endless supply of kerosene in one of the caves, which had been set up as a storeroom. It also contained cardboard boxes, stacked in rows, which appeared to contain food and other supplies.

All in all it would make a nice holiday home, she thought, for a troll!

Bingham wandered around the caves muttering, 'Oh dear.'

Ralph just plonked himself down in one of the armchairs that had been conveniently arranged in the central cave and harrumphed a few times.

'There's no use calling for help,' Candy had told them on the helicopter ride. 'It's a private island, patrolled by security guards. And, anyway, you're a long way from nowhere.'

She'd also said, 'Joe just wanted to kill you all, but I talked him into keeping you alive and came up with the idea of your little retirement home.'

Looking at the venom in her eyes when she looked at Bingham, though, Clara thought it had probably been the other way round.

The helicopter took off with a distant clacking sound and then the silence in the cave was absolute, except for the trickle of the stream.

'Where in the world are we?' she wondered aloud, not expecting an answer.

'Papua New Guinea,' Bingham replied. Considering that they had been locked below decks the entire time at sea, it was a testament to his surprisingly good sense of direction. 'Or possibly closer to the northern coast of Australia. Maybe New Zealand, but I don't think we went that far south.'

'Might as well be Mars,' harrumphed Ralph.

'Did you give them the correct formula?' Clara asked.

Bingham nodded. Ralph grunted, 'Did we have any choice?'

She shook her head slowly. 'No. No, I guess we didn't.'

Clara wandered around, inspecting their rocky home, then idly opened a few of the cardboard boxes of stores to find out the contents. The first one she tried contained packets of soup in a variety of flavours. The second contained canned meat.

She opened a third carton and began, a little tiredly, to laugh. Even here, trapped underground for the rest of her life in a tiny rock-walled prison, she was able to see the humour in the delicious irony of Candy's final revenge upon her ex-husband.

Ralph and Bingham crowded around her to see what was so amusing, but they didn't find it funny at all. Not even slightly.

The carton was full of cans of Coca-Cola.

STORM RISING

If all the Coca-Cola ever made was poured into bottles and lined up in a row, it would stretch from the earth to the moon over a thousand times. That's a lot of Coke.

Every second of every hour of every day, 8000 glasses of Coke gurgle down thirsty throats around the world. That's also a lot of Coke.

Coca-Cola was the first soft drink to be drunk in space.

Even the modern image of Santa Claus was actually invented by The Coca-Cola Company as part of its advertising campaigns in the first half of the twentieth century.

Tupai and Fizzer had learned all these very interesting facts, and many more, during their guided tour of Coca-Cola World with the acting CEO of The Coca-Cola Company, Reginald Fairweather.

And all of them, Tupai thought, he would trade in a second for a book on how to pick handcuffs.

'There are two things that worry me,' Fizzer said slowly, twisting his hands around inside the cuffs to see if there was any way to slide them off. (There wasn't.)

'Only two things?' said Tupai a little grimly.

'The first thing is: what are they going to do with us? And the second thing is, how did they know?'

'How did they know what?'

'That we were on the right track.'

Tupai thought about that for a moment, but it was all a little confusing, so he waited for Fizzer to explain.

Fizzer did, after a while. 'I think we know who, so that's not a question, it's the same people who kidnapped the three executives. Nothing else makes any sense. And I think we know why. We must have been getting too close to the correct recipe. But, at the moment, the only people who know the correct recipe, we assume, are the kidnappers, who will have wormed it out of the executives by now.'

'Or tortured it out of them,' Tupai said darkly, which wasn't like him, but then he'd never been handcuffed and left in a dimly lit room in the middle of heaven-knows-where before.

'But how did the kidnappers know that we were getting close to getting it right?'

'There's a spy inside The Coca-Cola Company,' Tupai said slowly.

'Yes,' said Fizzer, 'and that's what worries me the most, because, even within Coca-Cola, very few people know what is going on.'

'I think I'm more worried about the first question.' Tupai shifted his bulky frame around, trying to get comfortable, which was impossible on the hard concrete floor. 'What are they going to do with us?'

'I imagine they'll have to kill us,' Fizzer said, as if solving an algebra equation. 'Maybe not straight away, but if they let us go, sooner or later I would come up with the recipe, and I have a feeling that they don't want that to happen.'

'So why not just kill us straight away?'

'I don't know.' Fizzer ran his fingers through his longish hair. 'I think the penalty for murder in Georgia is the electric chair. It often is in these southern states.'

'Let me at the kidnappers and I'd save them some electricity,' Tupai rumbled. 'But if they're not going to kill us straight away, then *when*?'

'I don't know that either. I suppose they could always lock us in a cellar with a few weeks' supply of food and water, and when that was gone …'

He didn't have to say the rest, Tupai thought, and it didn't sound like a nice way to die. He looked around the dim room. The walls were made of large stones. It did look a bit like a cellar, he decided. And over in the corner were a few cardboard boxes.

A few weeks' supply of food.

A light but strong-looking chain wound through his handcuffs, through Fizzer's and around a stout wooden post in the centre of the room.

'We need to confront the board,' Fizzer said. 'If I can look in their eyes and ask them if they're involved, I think I'll know if someone's lying.'

Tupai held up his manacled hands. 'That's not going to be quite as easy as it sounds, or have you forgotten where we are?'

Fizzer shook his head. 'We know where we want to be; we know where we are now. All we have to do is work out how to get from here to there. A journey of a thousand miles begins with a single step.'

'Some days,' Tupai said, 'I wish you'd give up this airy-fairy crap and just come back down to reality.'

But there was a smile on his face as he said it.

The light in the room had grown measurably over the last twenty minutes or so, most of it coming from a high ventilation grille, only a few centimetres across. The light enabled them to get a better view of their surroundings. The floor was scattered here and there with mutterings of straw. At the far end of the room a short wooden flight of stairs led to a pair of heavy doors, not upright, as you would expect, and not horizontal, like trapdoors. They were on a steep slant, confirming the view that this was some kind of cellar.

Galloping horse hooves sounded distantly, the sound trickling down through the slots of the ventilation grille. The sound approached, then faded away again. A few moments later it repeated.

'We're on a farm somewhere,' Tupai said.

'A ranch, I think,' Fizzer said. 'A racing stable. I think that horse is galloping around a track.'

As if to prove him right, the sound approached again, then faded as before.

'Do they do much racing in Atlanta?' Tupai asked.

'Maybe we're not in Atlanta any more. I think we're still in Georgia though.'

'Your intuition again, right?'

'Maybe.' Fizzer pulled at his handcuffs absent-mindedly. 'And I seem to remember that if you cross a state line, the crime becomes a federal offence. I think that's worse somehow.'

'OK, so what do we know? We're handcuffed to a pillar, in a cellar ...'

'A tornado shelter,' interrupted Fizzer suddenly, his eyes on the heavy wooden doors on the other side of the room. 'That's what this is, it's a tornado shelter.'

'OK, a tornado shelter, out in the countryside somewhere, a hundred miles from civilisation for all we know, but probably still in Georgia. How's that going to help us when the food runs out?'

Fizzer didn't know. He pulled his harmonica out of his pocket instead of answering and started playing the traditional song of the southern states: Dixie. The mood lifted immediately.

Tupai laughed and sang along for a few bars.

'Oh, I wish I was in the land of cotton.

Old times there are not forgotten.

Look away, look away,

Look away Dixie Land.'

They ate cold beans out of a pull tag can that night and slept as well as they could by piling up some of the loose straw to make crude mattresses.

In the morning, with the effects of whatever had been in the water now fully worn off, and with the benefit of a little sleep, Fizzer finally had an idea.

Tupai had moved over to the heavy storm doors at the entrance to see if they looked as if they could be opened. He came back shaking his head.

'Built to withstand a tornado all right. You'd need a battering ram to get through those.'

Fizzer was hardly listening. He was watching the way the long chain had dragged across the edge of the centre post when Tupai had moved to the doors, splintering and chipping the wood.

'What's holding up the roof?' Fizzer asked.

'A great, big post,' Tupai said, in a kindergarten voice.

'And if we took the post away?'

'The roof would probably cave in and kill us.'

'Or it might cave in and leave a big hole we could climb out of. And if we stayed by the walls we could probably avoid being crushed.'

'Right,' said Tupai cheerily. 'So all we need is an axe.'

'Or a band saw,' Fizzer said quietly.

Half an hour later they had succeeded in knocking an edge off the post, about knee height. An hour later it had grown to a small indentation in the wood.

A chain does not make a very good band saw. Even so, by that night they had a groove about half a centimetre deep.

They took a dinner break at about six o'clock.

'This is going to take forever.' Tupai shook his head doubtfully, chewing over a mouthful of cold beans.

'Got anything better to do?'

By the end of the third day the groove was a deep cut. Tupai had one end of the chain, and Fizzer the other. They sawed away at the post by pulling the chain back and forth between them.

Progress was faster on the fourth day. The chain now slotted into the cut in the wood, and they didn't have to spend quite so much time or energy trying to keep it in position.

Two days after that, they were wholeheartedly sick of cold canned beans, but the post was cut almost to the middle.

'You'd have thought they could have varied the diet a little,' Tupai complained.

'Hmm.' Fizzer wrinkled his nose. 'Give me a box of matches and we could blow our way out of here.'

It was about noon on the Monday, after more than a week of imprisonment, when Tupai decided he'd had enough.

'I think I can break it,' he said.

Fizzer looked doubtful. The post was only two-thirds cut.

'If we push from the cut side,' Tupai explained, 'the weight of the post will help crack the timber on the other side. Then we push from the other side, and the weakened post should break.'

'We'll try it,' Fizzer agreed. 'What do I do?'

'Put your shoulder into it.'

Tupai sat on the floor and placed his feet on the post, just above the cut. Fizzer put his shoulder against the post, a little higher.

'Here goes nothing,' he said.

The post creaked and cracked and bent, until the gap they had cut had completely closed. It would give way no more after that.

They changed sides and pushed back but, despite their best efforts, they could only move the post a couple of centimetres before it sprang back to where it was.

Fizzer looked doubtfully at the cut, now completely closed up again.

'Maybe we should have waited a little longer,' he said.

There was no accusation in his voice, just a simple statement of fact.

'Sorry,' Tupai said.

'That's all right mate, we'll have a break now and make a new start in the morning.' Fizzer sat down on his haunches and wiped his forehead with the back of his wrist. 'Why is it so hard this way, when it was so easy the other way?'

'I think it's because we're now pushing against the weight of the wood. I didn't consider that before.'

Tupai sat down on the floor again and put his feet back up on the post. 'Half the problem is that I've got nothing to push against. If my back was up against the wall, I'd push against that.'

'I can be a wall,' said Fizzer.

Tupai looked at him questioningly.

'I can be a wall,' Fizzer repeated with conviction. 'It's just mind over matter.'

'Worth a crack,' Tupai said, although he wasn't sure that it was.

Fizzer sat back to back with Tupai and braced his feet against the wall of the cellar. 'I'll tell you when,' he said.

Tupai rested his feet on the post and waited. Fizzer's breathing began to slow. It was a kind of self-hypnosis. His back began to stiffen against Tupai's. An aura of calmness settled around him. Fizzer was becoming a wall.

Finally, Fizzer said quietly, 'Try now.'

Tupai braced his back against Fizzer's, and it was just like bracing against a concrete block wall. Fizzer's breathing continued, slow and measured, as it did when he was meditating.

Tupai's legs flexed and rippled and the post began to move. The 'wall' behind him was as solid as rock. He closed his eyes and clenched his fists and the post moved further, and further, until there was a crack and the half cut joint gave way completely, the weight of the post pulling it out of the ceiling mount. It would have crashed down on top of them, if Tupai hadn't deflected it with a powerful sweep of his arms.

It smashed into the side of the wall with a loud thud. Tupai helped Fizzer to his feet and they scanned the ceiling hopefully.

'How'd I do?' Fizzer asked.

'Solid, mate,' Tupai replied with affection. 'Solid as a rock.'

Unfortunately so was the ceiling. Apart from a slight sag in the long beams and a small fall of earth from between some of the cracks, the ceiling looked as solid as before.

'Well, it seemed like a good idea at the time,' Fizzer began.

Tupai was looking at the fallen post. It was a solid square-cut piece of timber, hewn from a single log. Knotholes showed here and there down its length.

'Do you remember what I said we'd need to open those doors?' he asked slowly.

Fizzer nodded. 'A battering ram.' His eyes landed on the post.

It took just six blows to smash the timber beam that braced the doors from the outside, then Tupai shouldered one of them open and they emerged blinking into a blue dome world.

'One more day living underground and I think I'd have gone mad,' Tupai said.

Tupai had no intuitive ability at all, as far as he knew, but it turned out to be a strangely prophetic statement for all that, and one that he would live to regret. But that didn't happen till much, much later.

THE UGLY BROTHERS

In the distance, beyond a fence and a grove of trees, they saw a mud track, probably the horse-training track they had heard being used on a number of occasions during their stay in the cellar. It was deserted now.

Tupai started to walk in that direction but Fizzer grabbed his arm and pointed to an axe, embedded in a stump, outside a nearby barn. A half-pitched haystack sat next to a long wooden-railed fence.

It took a single blow from Tupai to sever the short chain between Fizzer's handcuffs, and just four from Fizzer to sever Tupai's. Then, apart from a pair of iron bracelets each, they were free.

'Now what?' Tupai asked, but that question was answered for them as two young men, brothers by the look of them, came around the corner of the barn. The front one, the youngest, looked about eighteen. He carried a pitchfork and was obviously in the middle of doing something with the stack of hay.

They were about the same height, tall, with a lanky stride, and a flat-top, US Marines style haircut. Both wore the armless overalls Americans call dungarees. Neither would have carved out a successful career as a male model. Not by a long shot.

'Uh oh,' said the younger one, in a coarse southern accent

that was chalk and cheese to the relaxed Atlanta drawl of the city dwellers. 'Lookee like the rats is got outta the trap. Better sort that out afore Bobby gits ornery.'

His brother agreed. 'It ain't a good thang when Bobby gits ornery.'

Ugly Brother the Younger thrust the sharp end of the pitchfork at them as if fending off a wild animal. 'Back in yer hole, rats, back in yer hole.'

The older one laughed and the younger one grinned stupidly at them until Tupai took the pitchfork off him and broke it over his knee.

Just for clarification, he didn't just hand over the pitchfork with a nod and a smile, although Tupai had asked him for it reasonably politely considering the circumstances. The young man sat down in the pile of hay he had been pitching, blood streaming from his nose, while Tupai snapped the end off the pitchfork and tossed the pole to Fizzer.

The older brother looked a bit shell-shocked at that, and he wasn't the one who had been hit in the face with a power hammer, which is what Tupai's fist must have felt like. Maybe he was shocked at the sight of someone breaking a pitchfork across his knee (which is not exactly easy to do).

'Hell in a bucket, Curtis,' the older one said. 'What'd'ya let him hit yer fer?'

Curtis stood back up then, and, to use an American phrase, he was madder'n a cut snake.

Tupai stood still, clenching and unclenching his fists. You need to understand that Tupai had been learning the art of diplomacy over recent months. Frequently, he had found ways to avoid a fight, rather than charging in full throttle.

But he'd just spent a week and a bit in a storm cellar, eating nothing but cold beans, sawing at a wooden post with a length of chain. He wasn't exactly in a diplomatic mood. In fact Tupai was feeling downright ornery.

Fizzer swung the pole a couple of times around his back and shoulders. It was a bit heavy, a bit long, but it would do for a bo at a pinch. We can handle these two, he thought.

'Bobby,' the older one called, 'them fellas is escaped ferm the twister shelter.'

The door of the barn opened in a rush and big brother came out. He was wearing a cowboy hat and had a metal belt buckle with the Harley Davidson logo on it.

That wasn't Bobby though, nor was the next one who might have been a twin of the first, although that was nothing to be proud of. Bobby was the last one out, the oldest, the biggest and the ugliest member of the family, and that was saying something, as they weren't exactly The Backstreet Boys.

'So yer got out, did yer?' Bobby drawled, and spat on the ground in front of him. 'Well, I know some people ain't gonna be too happy about that. What did they tell me to do?'

He paused and stared for a moment at the ground, thinking, or maybe just looking for his spit.

Fizzer hefted the bo and shifted his weight forward on to his toes.

Bobby looked up. 'Oh, ah remember now. They tole me ter cut out yer tongue.'

A long utility knife appeared suddenly in his hand from a sheath on his belt.

'Guess I'd better earn ma pay check.'

He was big, gangly, wide across the shoulders and strong in

a kind of loose-limbed way. He was fast too. He stepped forward quickly, trying to grab the bo away from Fizzer with his free hand, the knife held dangerously in his other.

Fizzer spun the bo back out of Bobby's reach and gave him a tap on the side of his head for good measure. Then Tupai stepped in and grabbed the knife arm, and a fierce struggle developed as Bobby tried to avoid having his arm twisted slowly around and up behind his back.

Despite the age and height advantage, Bobby was no match for the squat, stocky packet of power that was Tupai White.

The four other brothers watched in amazement as a teenager twisted their senior sibling into submission.

Tupai twisted a little further, and Bobby gasped. The knife slid out of his hand. Tupai caught it and tossed it to one side, where it vanished into the depths of the haystack.

That broke the spell on the other ugly brothers and they all charged in at once. The bo flashed, and the first twin found his feet weren't where they ought to be. He dived face-first into a deposit from the horse bank.

The other twin caught the back swing from the bo on the side of his head and dropped groggily to his knees.

There were five of them, ranging from Curtis at about eighteen, to Bobby, probably nearing his thirties. They were all big, strapping American lads, raised on a diet of beef burger and rawhide. But they had never met a pair like Fizzer Boyd and Tupai White.

Fizzer found, in a series of whirling darts and jabs, that a bo was a great leveller of the odds against a bunch of people armed with just their fists.

Add into that equation Tupai White, who had grown up learning some nasty lessons on the back streets and rugby fields of Glenfield, and it was a very one-sided fight indeed.

There were more of them, but Tupai had fists like wrecking balls, which left them doubled up and gasping.

They tried to grab him and pin him, but he'd twist and break their grips, and again there would be a flurry of those demolition blows.

And, all the time, there was the swishing noise of the bo, and the thwock sound of hard wood meeting ugly brother.

Of the five, only Bobby was still standing when it was all over, and that was only because the back of his jacket had caught on an old nail on the side of the barn and kept him propped there on legs that had turned to hay stalks.

'Let's get out of here,' Tupai said, breathing heavily.

Fizzer found that he had barely raised a sweat. The practical application of all his training had seemed so natural, so effortless.

'I'm with you,' he said. 'Should we tie them up or something?'

'Nah,' Tupai said. 'Let's just find us some civilisation and send the police over. They've got nowhere to run to, they live here.'

The two of them turned towards the racetrack and started walking. It was the wrong decision, but how was Tupai to know the brothers had a shotgun?

Or two.

ANASTASIA BORKIN

Anastasia Borkin was very good at her job, and that job was harder than you might think. There was Executive Protection, Plant Security, Internal Security and, of course, Anti-Espionage, or Counter-Intelligence as she liked to call it, using an old spy term.

Industrial espionage was a growing problem in the US, partly thanks to the proliferation of small electronic devices that could convey voice and/or video, yet were small enough to hide in a cufflink or lapel badge.

Like anyone who was very good at her job, but had two major disasters on her hands, Borkin was fuming, angry mostly with herself, but also with anyone who she felt wasn't doing their job to the absolute best of their abilities.

Any of her staff seen shirking off home before the early hours of the morning were traitors in her view.

The Mad Russian, her staff had always called her, when she wasn't around, but it had been an affectionate term. Now they were using the nickname in a totally different way. She was mad all right, she was downright furious.

Anastasia Borkin strode the length of the boardroom, unable to sit still in one place while the world was exploding around her. First the disappearance of three of the executives it was her responsibility to protect, and then the kidnapping of the two young New Zealanders they had brought in.

What was worse, she suspected they had a spy somewhere in the company. That meant tracking down everybody who knew the results of the taste testing, and anyone they might have told about it, intentionally or accidentally, and anyone *they* might have spoken to, and so on.

And she couldn't let anyone know what was going on, not anyone. The whole thing had to be done with the delicacy of a brain operation, so as not to alert the spy that they were looking for him, or her.

Careless spies made mistakes, but spies who knew that hunters were on their trail, shut down their operations and were very careful not to make mistakes.

She had liked the two boys, which made the second kidnapping a whole lot worse. She had thought that Fizzer had a certain quality, of calmness and peace, which reached out and touched the people around him. Fizzer was destined for something big as an adult, she felt. And Tupai had a huge open smile and a wondrous enjoyment of life that was infectious.

But now they were also missing, and might even be dead for all she knew, and she was partly responsible.

'We need a little more time,' she thundered, wondering why the board couldn't see sense.

'There is no more time,' hot-blooded Ricardo lashed straight back at her. 'Either we start mixing today or we start running out of syrup.'

'We'll find them,' Borkin continued as if Ricardo hadn't spoken. 'We, and we includes both local and state police, and the FBI, have been door-to-door every day. We've found eye-witnesses who can trace the car as far as Macon.'

'What's in Macon?' Dolores asked, puzzled.

'Nothing, unless you count Cannonball House and the Confederate Museum,' Terry said.

'Which,' Borkin said, 'makes it a good place to hide the two boys.'

Keelan looked up from a sheet of figures. 'Or bury them.'

Borkin sank into her chair, and there was a general commotion around the table until Reginald held up a hand for quiet.

'We asked them to come and help us,' he said quietly, 'and they did, no questions asked. We're knee-deep in something, and we don't know what it is, and because of that, because of us, those two boys are in a whole world of trouble.'

Ricardo cracked his knuckles loudly, and Reginald glared at him. Was there more than mere annoyance behind the expression, Borkin wondered, reading the subtle body language of the acting CEO.

'And I liked those kids. Fizzer reminds me a bit of myself at his age, although he's a damn sight more together and sure of himself than I ever was. He has good qualities. They both do.'

There was a silence. Reginald resumed. 'But, whatever we feel about them, we can't base the future of this company on your chances of finding them, no disrespect Anastasia. I'm afraid I agree with Ricky, we have to start those vats boiling, and if 733-23-B is the best we've got, then that is what we are going to have to go with.'

'The public won't accept it,' Dolores said.

'The public will have to accept it,' Ricardo raged, 'because the alternative is no Coke at all!'

'I can find them,' Borkin interjected, but by that time nobody was listening.

The debate rolled and crashed like a thunderstorm for the next two hours, before they finally took a vote.

It was close, but the decision was final. That night the great vats in three massive factories, in three different countries, began to churn.

SHOTGUNS AND RATTLESNAKES

They had crossed over the racing track and were following a dusty metal road that led away from it when Fizzer heard the pick-up truck.

At first he thought that help was at hand, but then realised the noise was coming from behind them.

'Get off the road!' Fizzer said urgently, his intuition buzzing. Tupai, who had heard nothing, obeyed without question.

A row of small bushy shrubs ran the length of the road and they dived into it, disregarding a few scratches and cuts, just a half-second before a large khaki-coloured pick-up truck slid around the end of the road and spurted down past them, gravel flying from under its wheels.

An arm hung out of the driver's window, but the driver was looking the other way so they couldn't see his face.

The two men standing in the back of the pick-up were unmistakeable though, hanging on to the bucking frame with one hand and pointing shotguns in the air with the other. It was the ugly twins, and they looked uglier than ever.

Fizzer and Tupai crawled on their hands and knees behind the shrubs. It was one thing to be brave when faced with a pitchfork, but quite another kind of bravery to face up to a shotgun. The kind of bravery they award medals for, posthumously.

The shrubs, which made a kind of hedge, offered quite good concealment, so they followed them until the road turned a corner and the shrubs abruptly stopped.

There was no other cover, apart from the occasional tree, anywhere nearby.

'What do we do?' Tupai whispered from behind Fizzer.

'Wait,' Fizzer said.

'What for?'

'Night.'

They sat for a while, and Tupai even lay down for a time in the relative safety of the small hedge.

'Get some sleep,' Fizzer said. 'It'll be a long night.'

'How about you?'

'I'll be all right. You get some kip, I'll keep an eye out for Curtis and the Brothers Grimm.'

And Tupai did sleep.

In the bowels of the three factories, in Ireland, Africa and Puerto Rico, ingredients were sliding down massive stainless steel chutes into huge mixing and boiling vats by the time Tupai and Fizzer finally ventured out on to the metal road.

A car started nearby, and Fizzer froze, one hand back in warning, but the car drifted off somewhere in the distance.

They started to walk, navigating by starlight, conscious of the sound of their breathing and the crunch of their footsteps on the unsealed road. They travelled about a kilometre, without speaking, before Fizzer said, 'Sorry I dragged you into this, Tupai.'

Tupai placed a hand on his friend's shoulder in the dark. 'Wouldn't have missed it for the world, mate.'

A few more paces, then bright lights appeared in the distance burning fiery holes in the dark fabric of the countryside, and they heard the far-off sound of an engine.

'Down,' hissed Fizzer.

They scuttled off the road, dropping into a drainage ditch, mostly dry fortunately, which ran the length of the road.

The lights intensified until they could see two headlights, with a row of spotlights mounted on a rack above.

They buried their faces in the mud and weeds as the lights swept over their heads, but the vehicle did not slow. Fizzer looked up as it flashed past and saw a pick-up truck, although he could not tell from the back, in the dark, what colour it was, or who was driving it. They waited until it was a few hundred metres away before they crawled back out of the ditch and resumed their trek.

'Do you think it was them?' Tupai asked.

Fizzer shrugged. 'Better safe than sorry.'

After a moment Tupai asked, 'How do you know we're heading the right way?'

The answer came back with a grin Tupai could hear but not see in the darkness. 'We're heading away from the ranch. That's the right way.'

The truck, or a similar one, patrolled the road three or four times that night. A smaller vehicle, a car of some kind, passed them twice, and a loud Harley Davidson motorcycle breezed past once, the throaty roar of its engine unmistakeable from a long way off. Each time they took refuge in the ditch, and continued onwards as soon as the vehicle had passed.

One thing they realised, as the night progressed, was the sheer scale of everything in America. As light began to rise again over a range of hills to the east, the roads they had been following seemed no closer to ending than when the two had set out.

A tall row of poplars followed the road now, a windbreak for some barns and other smaller buildings now appearing out of the darkness with the coming of the dawn.

'We'd better get off the road again,' Fizzer said, eyeing the buildings with suspicion. They didn't seem populated, or even dwellings, but if they were work buildings then they could attract visitors during the day.

'Have we passed a McDonalds yet?' Tupai asked as they slipped through the poplars. 'Isn't there supposed to be one around every corner in America?'

Fizzer nodded. 'I'd even settle for a Burger King.'

'Double whopper with cheese.'

'Large fries and onion rings.'

'Nope, lay off the onion. You've been eating canned beans for a week, the resulting explosion could be catastrophic.'

'True.'

'But a chocolate shake for dessert.'

'Strawberry and banana mixed.'

'Chocolate.'

'Strawberry-banana.'

The other side of the trees was scrubland, green-brown grass and clumps of thorny weeds. A few metres away, a thicket of wild cane stretched along another fence. Behind it was a freshly ploughed field, where a massive metal plough and the tractor that pulled it rested in the half-light of the early morning.

They slept after a while from sheer exhaustion. The poplars provided shade, for the morning at least. They never made it to the afternoon, their peaceful slumber was brutally stolen by the sound of trotting hooves. The sound came, not from the road side of the poplars, but from the scrubland side where they were lying.

'Follow me,' Fizzer whispered, shaking Tupai awake, and they sprinted across the uneven ground to the cane thicket, pushing aside the stalks and making a path as deep inside as they could.

Fizzer, who was in front, looked behind to see Tupai quietly, but systematically, straightening and steadying the cane stalks behind them to conceal their passage.

The hooves sounded closer, and something slithered across the ground past Tupai's feet.

'Do they have rattlesnakes in Georgia?' he whispered.

'I don't know,' came the unhelpful response.

The hooves stopped at the cane thicket and a stick, or maybe a shotgun, began to beat the first few clumps. Whoever it was didn't venture into the thicket though, and the sound of the hooves started again and gradually faded.

'Why didn't they check it out properly?' Fizzer wondered.

'Perhaps they know about the rattlesnakes,' Tupai said with concentrated coolness, as there was another slithering sound near his ankles. 'Watch where you step on the way out.'

'You don't want to stay in here? In case they come back.'

'In a word, no.'

They both trod very carefully on their way out of the thicket, and the slithering sounds kept a safe distance from them, or at least they didn't get bitten.

'I suppose we should make a start,' Fizzer said, looking both ways down the narrow lane. 'No point in waiting around here for him to come back.'

Tupai shook his head. 'Nah. I'm sick of this sneaking around. And we don't know how far we have to go. We could be walking for weeks.'

'So your suggestion is?'

'We go for a tractor ride.'

Fizzer swung round and looked at the tractor sitting idle in the middle of the field.

'What's it doing there, do you think?'

'I'd say whoever is supposed to be driving that thing is too busy looking for us.'

'So we just hop on, start her up and make a run for it?'

Tupai nodded.

'Simple as that?'

'Simple as that.'

Of course it wasn't.

THE TRACTOR GREEN

Tupai managed to start the tractor all right, that part was easy, and Fizzer had driven one before, when his father had a job as a farm manager on a sheep station in the middle of the North Island. So they were soon rolling, heading towards an open gate at the far end of the field. First Fizzer had had to work out how to lift the plough, a solid metal apparatus attached to the back of the tractor, with sharp-looking tines curving down into the soil.

The plough rose and flattened itself against the rear of the tractor when Fizzer finally found the right lever.

They rumbled slowly across the field and out on to the road, where the tractor was able to pick up quite a good speed, the large rubber tyres with the deep tread making a buzzing noise on the hard metal of the road.

'Le tracteur vert,' Tupai shouted with a smile over the noise of the engine and the tyres.

'Le what?' Fizzer looked back at him, perplexed.

'I never paid much attention in French,' Tupai shouted, 'but for some reason I remember that phrase, le tracteur vert. The tractor green.'

For some reason this seemed really funny, and they both laughed for a while. It felt good not to be walking, and it felt good to be making some real progress. They must have been travelling at around thirty kilometres per hour, which was all the tractor could manage.

The sun warmed their backs and the breeze of their speed ruffled their hair. It was altogether a much more pleasant feeling than lying face down in a muddy ditch.

The ugly brothers spotted them as they passed a grassy track that led to another huge barn. The pick-up truck was circling around in front of the barn when there was a shout from one of the brothers on the back of it, and it suddenly accelerated back down the track towards the road. It was a small satisfaction to see one of the twins lose his footing when the truck took off and slide back down the tray, cracking his head on the tailgate.

The pick-up slid out of the track on to the road, sending shingle flying, and came charging after them like a dog after a wild pig.

As it spun out of the track they could see the other twin aiming a shotgun in their direction, but then the truck was behind them, hidden by the metallic mass of the plough.

The plough was keeping them alive. On one side of the road was the drainage ditch, on the other a sturdy wooden fence. The plough was wide enough to block the small dirt road, leaving no room for the pick-up truck to pass. And it was solid enough to block any shots the brothers might be stupid enough to make.

There was a bang behind them, and a spray of pellets bounced harmlessly off the underside of the plough.

Fizzer and Tupai's estimate of the brothers' intelligence dropped a few more points. A couple more shots rebounded from the metal behind them but none penetrated the thick steel.

The pick-up truck swerved to the left, then to the right, as if by doing so it could find a way past.

An open gate appeared in front of them, opening on to another freshly ploughed field, huge furrows running the length of the paddock.

On impulse, Fizzer swung the big machine in through the gate and across the field of dirt. As he'd hoped, the pick-up truck slid to a halt at the gate, the narrow tyres of the truck unable to cope with the soft dirt and deep ruts of the freshly ploughed field.

The tractor trundled away happily, although the big tyres did score deep grooves sideways across the field, making a mess of someone's hard work.

The pick-up pulled forwards a few yards, trying to get an angle on the tractor, but Fizzer aimed the tractor away from them a little, blocking their shot with the plough until they were out of range.

Another gate on the far side of the field led to another road, tarsealed. Fizzer felt a rising hope. Tarseal. That surely meant a public road.

'I think we're getting close to civilisation,' he shouted.

On cue, the khaki pick-up screamed around the corner of a road somewhere behind them, its tyres smoking with anger as it slid on to the tarseal.

'This is not good,' Tupai shouted.

The road was wider, and there was just enough space for the truck to get by, if Fizzer would let it, so he didn't. He swung the tractor desperately from right to left as the truck swerved around behind them.

Tupai was examining the rig of the plough, holding on to the roll bar with two rigid hands as the machine careened along the road.

'I've got an idea,' he shouted. 'When I tell you to, slam on the brakes.'

Tupai reached up to the plough attachment. He had to stand on the seat of the tractor and stretch to his full height. The way the tractor was waltzing down the road made it almost suicidal.

Another pointless shot bounced off the underside of the plough as he reached up and pulled out a small locking bolt, then grasped the fat, rubber-coated handle of the assembly pin.

'Ready …' he shouted, watching the truck through a small gap in the plough and bracing himself with one hand on the roll bar. 'Now!'

Fizzer stood on the brakes. Literally. He stood up out of the seat with all his weight on one foot, the one on the brakes.

A tractor is a huge deadweight and takes a lot of stopping, but those massive tyres put a lot of rubber on the road and, when they stop turning, they grip like glue.

The tractor shrieked to a halt, smoke pouring from both big tyres, and slewed a little to one side.

The pick-up truck slammed its anchors on too, but not quickly enough, and it rammed into the back of the tractor between the great wheels. It was a fight the tractor won.

Even before the impact, Tupai wrenched out the huge pin with a sound that was half scream, half roar, and the whole weight of the plough smashed down on to the front of the pick-up, the metal tines scything through the hood and into the engine bay below, with a screeching, tearing sound.

'Go! Go!' Tupai yelled, and Fizzer stood on the accelerator. The tractor surged forward dragging the hood of the truck, the distributor cap, the carburettor, half the radiator and a collection of small plastic hoses and wires with it.

The whole mess hit the road as it was dragged forward off the pick-up and the rear end of the plough bounced out of the towing bars and gouged its way to a stop in the tarmac.

The tractor went a lot faster, they discovered, without the plough, and they took off down the road, leaving the ugly brothers staring at the wreck of their truck.

Ten minutes later a State Police Cruiser approached on the other side of the road, and, by a combination of arm signals and general mad shouting, they managed to get it to stop.

The troopers inside were tough, experienced front-line policemen, with handguns the size of small cannons strapped to their waists, and hats that looked a little like lemon squeezers.

More importantly, though, they had a photo of Fizzer and Tupai in a clipboard on their dash.

JOKE-A-COLA

The backlash was more widespread and vehement than anyone could have anticipated.

They began shipping the new formula that week, and most of the bottling plants around the United States, along with almost all the international plants, were using it a fortnight later when their existing syrup stocks ran out.

The response from the public was both immediate and frightening. There were public rallies in Pittsburgh, marches in Washington DC, and near riots in some areas of Los Angeles.

Coca-Cola denied the recipe had changed, although it was pretty obvious to anyone with tastebuds that it had.

Network news bulletins carried the news as a lead story, and even the normally sedate *New York Times* had a front page banner asking, 'Is this the Real Thing?'

Local channels interrupted daytime programming, including the popular soap, *The Beautiful Years*, to report the story, but that only caused a backlash against the channels from viewers for whom nothing less than World War Three would have justified interrupting the programme.

People began stockpiling older bottles, with the original formula, and a black market took off on the Internet with cans of 'Old Coke' selling for up to twenty times the price of the new product. Two US Congressmen came out swinging at The Coca-Cola Company, and a group of lawyers in Seattle filed a class-action suit to force Coca-Cola to change back.

What they didn't realise, of course, was just how impossible that was.

Critics called the drink, 'the Coke you have when you're not having a Coke'. David Letterman, on *The Late Show*, called it 'Joke-a-Cola', while Jay Leno on *The Tonight Show*, paraphrasing an old Coca-Cola advertising line, said, 'Things go better with … just about anything else,' before pouring a can of Coke down a toilet that had been set up on stage.

This caused a renewed outbreak of fury, directed, not at Jay Leno, who had done the pouring, but at The Coca-Cola Company, who had done the mixing.

There was something sacred, it seemed, about the century-old soft drink, something deeply embedded in the American psyche. Pouring Coke down a toilet was akin to burning an American flag, and the anger was real and extreme, as if the executives at The Coca-Cola Company were, somehow, trying to cheat the American public out of their heritage.

Nor was the raging storm limited to the United States. In Mexico and Iceland, the two largest per-capita drinkers of Coca-Cola in the world, cars were overturned and buses burned in some of the largest street riots seen in those countries. Particularly in Iceland, where rioting was a relatively unknown pastime. In Uruguay a seventy-year-old man chained himself to the top of a church steeple, claiming that he would not come down until they re-introduced the original recipe. In Rio de Janeiro a special Coca-Cola Carnival was held, in a strange kind of prayer to Coca-Cola to reconsider.

Coca-Cola stocks dropped. They plummeted in fact, faster than they had during the *New Coke* blunder of the 1980s, and there was no sign of the near miraculous recovery that had occurred back then, when they had simply reverted to the original flavour.

Most of this, Fizzer and Tupai learned from the newspapers that were delivered daily to their expensive suite at the Four Seasons hotel. Some of it they picked up from the television news, and other information came to them first hand in the shape of Anastasia Borkin, who visited them daily, partly to check on them and partly to check on the armed guards, who were rostered in shifts in the corridor outside their room. No point in taking chances, she thought.

The next day brought even more bad news for The Coca-Cola Company, when a major fast food restaurant chain announced it was breaking a long tradition of serving only Coca-Cola products, and would, in future, be supplying a cheaper Australian soft drink. This announcement followed hard on the heels of similar announcements from some major international airlines.

The day also brought more news from the FBI, which was handling the kidnapping charges that had been levelled against Robert, Leonard, Kenneth, Hank and Curtis Cooper, five brothers who ran a mixed ranch and racing stables in Macon, Georgia.

The Cooper brothers, it turned out, were well-known to the local law enforcement agency, and State Troopers had been on their way to investigate the farm when two idiots, yelling and screaming from the top of a large green tractor, had waylaid them.

The FBI had asked the boys to stay around until they could properly arraign the Cooper brothers, and The Coca-Cola Company was happy to foot the hotel bills, considering what they had put the lads through.

The Cooper brothers were not entirely co-operative, but a mixture of promises and threats in separate interviews had the FBI convinced that they were no more than hired muscle, paid to keep the two boys under lock and key.

All other things considered, the whole affair had been an unmitigated disaster. The taste tests were discontinued, as the only thing The Coca-Cola Company could be sure of, was that if changing the formula once had been a disaster, then changing it a second time would be a catastrophe, unless they could absolutely guarantee they had re-discovered the original recipe.

All efforts were directed into the search for the Coca-Cola Three, but this too had turned into a series of blind alleys and red herrings, and the investigation was treading water with no good leads.

The Coca-Cola Company, of course, paid Fizzer and Tupai the agreed hourly rate, but not the huge bonus they would have got for cracking the formula.

It was probably enough to cover Fizzer's university expenses, but it wouldn't get him and his dad out of the caravan, and Italian sports cars were definitely out of the question.

Within the boardroom of The Coca-Cola Company a furious debate was raging, which saw some of the most vitriolic speeches the walnut-lined walls had witnessed. Some of those present, including Anastasia Borkin, wanted to come clean with the American public and let them know of the kidnappings and the reason for the change in the formula.

'They'll sympathise,' she expounded, whenever she had the chance. 'They'll take pity on us and forgive us the new taste while we keep searching.'

Others wanted to continue to deny any change had occurred, as if it were just some collective fantasy.

'There are millions of Coke drinkers out there who are continuing to drink the new flavour,' was Ricardo's argument. 'We've already alienated the Coke fans. If we admit there really was a change, then all we'll do is alienate everyone else. Deny, deny, deny. We'll suffer, but we'll survive. Wash our dirty linen in public and we won't last out the year.'

Borkin thought Ricardo was more concerned about lasting out the year as Vice-President (Production) than he was about Coca-Cola, the Company, lasting out the year.

Eventually, of course, the arraignment took place, and, after signing affidavits, both Tupai and Fizzer were allowed to return home. First class, which was part of The Coca-Cola Company's way of saying sorry.

Borkin herself drove them to the airport, in her own private car. Somehow the brightly coloured company limousines seemed inappropriate for what was not a brightly coloured occasion.

The farewell was long and quite emotional, but she eventually watched them walk away through security to their waiting flight with an overwhelming feeling of guilt. Guilt born of seeing them arrive, excited and happy with their heads held high, and now to be sending them off home again. Defeated. Dejected. Disillusioned.

THE HEIMLICH MANOEUVRE

Sharron Palmer smiled sweetly at the two young men she had been asked to chaperone as she checked their tray-tables and seatbelts.

The shorter of the two hardly fitted into the airline seat, so broad were his shoulders. It was lucky they were flying first class, she thought, as the seats were considerably narrower back in economy.

They didn't look like her usual first class passengers and they didn't act like them either. First class passengers often had high expectations that were somehow always disappointed. Usually they made Sharron feel as though she were directly responsible for all the indignities they had to suffer in their fully reclinable, extra-sized, super-comfortable seats. They blamed her for the noise of the engines, filtered through the sound protection and insulation of the plane, that interfered with their enjoyment of the in-flight movies, which they considered to be very poorly selected and most unsuitable for playing on an aircraft.

These young men, on the other hand, found the first class cabin a source of amazement; even the buttons that made the seats go up and down seemed like something that had been put there just for their entertainment. A fact which appeared to grate on the nerves of the other passengers in the cabin.

However, looking at the disdainful expressions compared to the sheer youthful exuberance of the two boys, Sharron happily ignored the pointed looks and let the two have fun.

Later, she thought, she'd see if the captain would let them visit the flight deck. It wasn't as easy to arrange such things as it had been a few years ago, but she thought she could convince him.

After their initial enthusiasm for the gadgets and first class gimmicks, though, they settled down quietly, a little too quietly. There was an air of adventure about them, as though they had just been on one, but overlaid on that was a sadness, a feeling that things had not gone well. Sharron Palmer was pretty good at reading people after fifteen years of dealing with their little foibles and quirks, jammed in a tin can with them at thirty thousand feet for sometimes a day at a time. She often passed the flight times by guessing what was going on in their lives, behind the emotionless faces, make-up and coiffured hair.

White, T. and Boyd, F. as she read from the passenger manifest, had probably been to Disneyland, she decided, and maybe some of the rides had been shut.

Whoever was paying for their fares – and judging by their clothes, it wasn't their parents – had not asked for any special treatment, but Sharron felt that they deserved, and maybe even needed, a little looking after, so she made sure they had everything and then some.

It was about fourteen hours to Sydney, and then another four to Auckland after that. It was an odd dogleg of a flight but, as it was a Qantas flight, they routed through Sydney or Melbourne.

Sharron was tall – that was a requirement of the job for certain technical and safety reasons – she was blonde and she was bubbly. At least that was how most of her passengers would describe her to their families and friends; if indeed, they bothered to describe her at all, which most of them wouldn't. And bubbly, when used to describe Sharron, was not the insult that it could be when describing some other people. It wasn't a ditzy kind of bubbliness, for Sharron's eyes shone with an insightful intelligence. It was more the expression of an effervescent personality and a *life* that could not be contained. All of her passengers liked her, usually immediately they met her. Which didn't stop them from treating her like a labour-saving appliance.

The meals in first class were served on delicate looking, but robust, Wedgwood china. The forks and spoons were silver, although the knives were plastic, as required by law. The first class meals were both nutritionally excellent and, actually, quite delicious as well, and had won several airline cuisine competitions.

Dinner included cheese (Australian) and two salty crackers (also Australian). This fact may seem like mindless trivia, but was to become vitally important by the end of the meal.

Sharron paused at the seats of the two young men and with a smile asked, 'Can I get you two anything to drink? And don't ask for beer, because you're not old enough and I'd get in trouble.'

Tupai laughed. 'Just water for me, thanks, wouldn't want to get you in trouble.'

He was quite softly spoken. Somehow she had expected a rough, rasping voice to go with the burly frame.

The taller one smiled as well. 'I'll have a Coke, thanks.' Then, to no-one in particular, 'Might as well get it while it lasts.'

Water and coke, Sharron thought, pouring the drinks in the first class galley. Easily pleased, those two, unlike Mrs Scarborough in 2D who had requested a mixture of Champagne, Perrier, orange juice and brandy, and had rejected the drink twice as not being mixed in the right proportions.

The water came out of a sealed bottle, no airline tank water for first class passengers! The coke was Corker Cola, the only brand the airline now carried. It was good to support a local industry after all, and there was all that fuss at the moment over the taste of actual Coca-Cola.

She made her way, quietly and unhurriedly, as they were taught to do, back to the two boys, past the insistent mutterings of Hendren, E. in 1A, who thought that the bread roll was too cold, or hard or something.

'There you go,' she smiled, placing the water on one of the trays and the cola on the other. 'And there's plenty more if you want it. We won't run out.'

'No, no, that's not what I meant,' Boyd, F. said, with a small sad smile. 'I meant that pretty soon it's going to be impossible to get Coca-Cola at all. The real thing, I mean, not that new stuff. This is probably one of my last chances.'

'Oh.' She squatted down beside the seat for a moment to bring her head below his. They were taught to do that in first class as well. 'Well, in that case I have a small confession. We don't actually carry Coca-Cola any more. It's all Australian now.'

'Corker Cola?' he asked, with an expression of dismay.

'Sorry. Do you want something else?'

'No,' he said. 'That's OK. I wouldn't want to put you to any more trouble. You've been so nice.'

'Actually, you're the one who has been so nice,' she said, and meant it. 'You and your friend.'

'Fiz … Fraser,' he said. 'And this is my mate, Tupai.'

'Tupai. Is that Samoan?'

There was a quick exchange of glances between the two as if this happened a lot.

'Actually it's a Maori name. I'm half Maori and half Chinese.'

'Are you sure there's nothing else I can get you?'

'No,' Fizzer said, and Tupai shook his head. 'We're fine thanks.'

They demolished the meal, as two growing lads should; quite unlike Peckinshaw in 5B who barely touched it, and pronounced it inedible when she came to take the plate away.

The cola was untouched, she saw, as she passed Fraser, and if there had been any way to replace it with a Coca-Cola, even if she'd had one of her own in her personal bag, she would have.

Just as she passed, Fizzer erupted into a fit of coughing, crumbs and bits of cracker spraying over the back of the seat in front of him. She quickly turned to see if there was anything she could do. Once a passenger had actually started choking in her section. She had grabbed him up out of his seat and performed the Heimlich manoeuvre on him and saved his life.

This didn't seem that serious though, just a bit of cracker that had gone down the wrong way, she thought.

Fizzer coughed and pounded on his chest with his fist but waved a hand at her to show he was OK.

After a moment of throat clearing, he reached out and took the glass of Corker Cola to wash it all down. His face froze. He looked as if he were going into shock.

'Are you OK?' Sharron asked quickly, dropping Peckinshaw's plate to the ground, ready to do whatever she had to, to save this nice young man's life.

He nodded, turning slowly to look at her. He swallowed. Then he took another, longer sip from the glass. He pursed his lips and ran it around a few times inside his mouth before swallowing.

Finally, he said emphatically, 'This is not Corker Cola.' As if somehow he could tell the difference. 'It's Coca-Cola.'

Sharron shook her head, but he insisted and wouldn't believe her till she showed him the can.

CORKER, BONZER, DINKY DI

The Coca-Cola Company of Atlanta, Georgia, sued Corker Cola Aust. Pty Ltd., of Sydney, Australia, when they first launched their product, claiming that the name 'Corker Cola' was too close to the name of their own brand 'Coca-Cola' and therefore was in breach of the laws of 'Passing Off', which prevent one product from attempting to pass itself off as that of its competitor.

Corker Cola argued, successfully, that 'Corker' was a time-honoured Australian expression for 'Good, Great, Excellent or Jolly Well Done' and, therefore, was no more an example of 'passing off' than if they had called it, 'Bonzer Cola', 'Dinky Di Cola', or even 'Cracker Cola' although, in truth, that was more of a New Zealand expression.

It was an Australian judge.

A cold war had existed between the two companies ever since, and each had carved out its own share of the cola market. Coca-Cola took the high ground of purists, connoisseurs and the more discerning drinker, while Corker Cola won over the low ground of the bulk market and the price-conscious drinker; those who would drink anything black and bubbly providing it didn't come directly from the outflow of an aluminium smelter, and even that, providing it was cold enough.

Fizzer had never thought of Corker Cola as anything but a cheap Australian knock-off brand, but he looked at the company now from a whole new perspective: as kidnappers, spies, and possibly even murderers. It was a moderately disturbing point of view.

Since the fateful sip of cola on the Qantas flight for Sydney, a number of things had happened simultaneously, most of which Fizzer knew about, although there were a couple that he didn't.

Sharron, the flight attendant, who seemed to have adopted them since their arrival on board for no good reason other than the warmth of her own heart, was still up in the cockpit. She had been there on and off for the last twenty minutes trying to arrange an Extra-ordinary Departure for them in Sydney, which meant getting their tickets altered and their luggage off the plane.

'That's not really possible,' she'd said doubtfully when Fizzer had first asked, but he'd heard the word 'really' as meaning that it wasn't impossible and had implored her to ask someone, without telling her the reason why. The amount of time and effort she was now going to on their behalf quite astounded him, and he didn't understand why she was so accommodating, so caring.

The other thing he knew about was the activity now underway in Auckland, New Zealand. It was after hours, and the night duty receptionist at Coca-Cola Amatil had, at first, refused to connect his call to Harry Truman's mobile phone, citing privacy laws and company policy, but something in Fizzer's voice must have convinced her at least to phone Mr Truman and let him know who was calling him from an air-phone on a 747 in the middle of the Pacific Ocean. Harry had taken the call at once.

'I don't know who to trust,' Fizzer had started, 'except you.'

It had taken ten minutes of incredulous questions from Harry before Fizzer finally managed to bring him up to date with the astounding fact that Corker Cola had the secret formula, and give him instructions for what he needed him to do.

In Atlanta, Georgia, well beyond the scope of any intuitive powers that Fizzer might or might not have, Anastasia Borkin was preparing a trap. If she'd known what Fizzer was up to, she might have organised things differently, but her psychic powers were no stronger than his.

And on another 747, in the middle of the Pacific Ocean, Dennis Cray, fourth dan karate black belt, mountain climber, blackwater diver and bojutsu expert, was feeling like anything but the toughest man in the world, no matter what his students might think of him.

The 100 man kumite had been harder than he could have dreamed. Fighting one hundred karate opponents of varying levels of skill, one after the other, he had discovered, could really knock the stuffing out of you. The bruises and welts that covered his body would be there for weeks, and he was fairly sure that he had cracked his left radius, the smaller of the two bones in his forearm. That was not a major problem in itself, as the ulna, the larger of the two bones, would act as a natural splint while its little cousin healed.

Dennis had the 'Golden Oldies' channel selected on the music system, and the Beach Boys' 'Surfin' Safari' was blaring out as loud as he could get it without annoying the lumpy woman in the unusual red felt dress seated next to him. Surfin' Safari reminded him of Reiko, the beautiful Japanese girl who had been one of the adjudicators on the kumite panel. That made no sense at all, because surfing in 1960's California was about as far removed from modern day karate tournaments in Japan as it was possible to get. But then again, everything reminded him of Reiko at the moment.

Reiko was to join him in New Zealand in a couple of months, and they had a month-long holiday planned, most of which would be spent either high in the air, astride a snow-capped mountain, or deep under the earth, with a little bungee jumping and high-speed jet boating thrown in for light relief. Reiko, incredibly, shared the same outdoor interests as he did.

Life was looking good at the moment, Dennis thought. The only thing that had dampened his mood just a little was the fact that his direct flight to Auckland had been cancelled due to bad weather and he had been rescheduled on an alternative flight, with a four-hour stopover in Sydney.

THE LOST RECIPE

Anastasia Borkin bustled into the meeting late, leaving the featureless security guard to close the door behind her.

That, in itself, was cause for some consternation among the other Vice-Presidents, as Borkin had never been late for a meeting before, or, in fact, for anything else in her life.

The lateness was deliberate, however, and she allowed herself the tiniest of smiles as she settled in her plush, leather, executive-quality boardroom chair. She had waited in a cubicle in the ladies' toilets until five minutes after the meeting had started. The unexpected lateness, she knew, would add credibility to what she was going to say, and credibility was going to be paramount. If the targets of her charade believed her, she would have them hooked. If they suspected she was lying, they'd shut down everything, and she might never find out who they were.

Worse, if they panicked, then their accomplices, who were holding the three missing executives, might also panic, and clean up all loose ends. Which would include Clara Fogsworth, Bingham Statham, and Ralph Winkler. Assuming, that was, they were still alive in the first place. They had to be alive, she reassured herself. Anything else was *unthinkable!*

So, it was a risk she was taking, but a calculated one.

Keelan had stopped talking when she walked in. He had been in the middle of a sentence but paused, waiting for her to sit.

She didn't let him finish.

'We have the recipe, the original recipe!' she exclaimed, her eyes rapidly scanning the reactions of those around the table. Surprise, uncertainty, hope. All understandable. No obvious shock, or panic. If the spy was at this table, as she believed, then he or she was a very good actor.

'How?' 'Where?' 'Who?' The questions came from all directions.

'A copy was kept, illegally of course, during the New Coke episode of the eighties, by an employee who thought that it would become a collector's item one day, never dreaming that we would switch back to the old recipe within a few months.' It sounded so plausible that Borkin almost believed it herself. She continued. 'I have guaranteed him immunity from any legal action, and he has agreed to send the recipe by immediate FedEx. It should be here this afternoon.'

That caused a commotion and it was a few minutes before she was able to answer Ricardo's first question.

'Why FedEx it? Why not fax it through?'

Borkin had thought of that. 'It's scribbled on the side of a cardboard box, an old Coke carton. It can't be faxed. Maybe he could have transcribed it, but I was afraid he could make an error, so I asked him to send the original.'

'Are you sure it's the correct recipe?' Keelan asked.

Actually she knew it was not. It was 733-23-A with a few changes in case anyone recognised it. She had copied it on to the box herself, then spent an hour rubbing the box on the carpet, standing on it, doing all she could to age it, before posting it to an old school friend in Ontario.

'Yes, I'm sure. The employee is adamant about it.'

'Who is it?'

'I can't reveal that. It's part of the agreement.'

Reginald said, 'I can't believe you entrusted this to FedEx! Do you have any idea how important this is? Why not send one of our people?'

'It's coming from Waterloo, Ontario,' Borkin said. 'We don't have anyone there. FedEx will be fast and safe, and in any case, it's already on its way.'

Still no panic or guilty reactions from anyone. Was she right? Why was she so sure it was one of the Vice-Presidents? At least ten other people in the company, technicians mainly, must have known the results of the taste tests.

Reginald nodded. 'All right. Let me know when it arrives. I want our top people to review it immediately and give an opinion on its authenticity.'

'Absolutely,' Borkin said.

The airport terminal was bigger than they expected. Sydney seemed on a different scale altogether to LAX, which they had flown into and out of, on their way to Atlanta. Tupai said it was because LAX was made up of several smaller terminals, whereas Sydney was just a single big building.

Fizzer had no idea whether Tupai was telling the truth or talking through a hole in his head. But it seemed plausible. Surely LA would have a bigger International Airport than Sydney?

Sharron had said goodbye and, in her most professional manner, had offered to shake Tupai's hand as they had disembarked. He'd taken her hand, but then, on impulse, those big arms had reached out and hugged her. Fizzer did the same, and he thought he'd seen a tear in her eye as they'd walked up the airbridge.

They were the first ones out and through Passport Control in record time. That turned out to be good luck in more ways than one because if they'd arrived at Baggage Claim just five minutes later they would never have run into Dennis.

'Fizzer! Tupai!' he called from across the other side of the luggage conveyor, startling an elderly Japanese couple.

'Sensei!'

That drew an intrigued look from the couple.

After some vigorous hand shaking, Dennis asked, 'Something's wrong. Are you two in trouble?'

Fizzer looked at Tupai, who nodded, before launching into an explanation of the disaster that had occurred and the clue they'd found on board the plane.

Dennis was a good head taller than Fizzer and another half taller than Tupai. He looked down at them and said, 'What can I do to help?'

The boys didn't take much persuading, and neither did the airline, which happily delayed his return flight to New Zealand.

Harry Truman made some carefully worded phone calls to a couple of people he felt he could trust beyond question. First he'd had to kick his sons off the Internet, where they'd been in a heavy-metal chat room, so that he could use the telephone.

Then he logged on to the Internet himself, and transferred a substantial amount of money to a friend of his in Sydney. He transferred it from his own personal account, as he had no access to company accounts and, anyway, would need two signatures on a form, which could not happen until the next business day, and which might raise some eyebrows he didn't want raised.

If all went well, he thought, he'd put an extraordinary expenses claim in to Huia in accounts. She'd bite his head off, but that was just one of the risks you took. If it all went bad, then he'd write off the money as 'the least he could do to help'. His sons waited impatiently for him to finish so they could resume their argument with someone in Finland over whether Metallica or Iron Maiden was the greatest heavy metal band of all time. Harry sighed as he logged off. It was the least he could do to help.

One of the people he had rung worked for Coca-Cola Amatil in Australia. He felt she could be trusted completely. The other was Mohammad Sarrafzadeh, an acquaintance of his, also in Sydney, who had nothing to do with The Coca-Cola Company, or the soft drink business in general. Mohammad's occupation was listed on his driver's licence as 'Research Consultant', which didn't really describe very well the work he did investigating fraud in large corporations.

Harry had thought very carefully about who he could ring, who he could trust. Fizzer had made it quite clear that if the wrong people learned what they were doing, they'd have to stop looking for three missing persons and start looking for three graves.

ATRIUM

Vice-President Borkin lay on the floor of room 202a of the Coca-Cola tower and watched the comings and goings through the main doors of the Corporate Headquarters just across the plaza.

It was a smallish office, much smaller and more spartan than her own, and she thought she kept hers fairly bare. Here, there were no pot plants, family photographs or personal knick-knacks, any of the individual stuff that made an office feel like home.

John Gregor, whose office it was, was on a long wild goose chase around the building, thanks to some inventive storytelling.

Her powerful binoculars brought the reception area so close that she felt she could reach out and touch it.

A few advertising agency types entered and waited at the reception desk until whisked away by someone from marketing. A few staffers left, heading out for what she couldn't imagine, unless they had appointments outside. They certainly weren't stepping out for coffee and bagels, as the best cafeteria in the whole of downtown Atlanta was situated on the top floor of the building she was lying in.

The carpet, which felt luxuriantly soft when you were in the usual position, i.e. standing on it, was starting to get spiky and scratchy against the skin of her elbows.

A tall man, head and shoulders above those around him, got out of a large white van and ducked his head as he walked through the doors of the building, three or four hangers-on hanging on around him. He turned in her direction for a moment and, in the crystal disc of the binoculars, she recognised him as a basketballer they were signing up for an endorsement package.

The van pulled away, but was almost immediately replaced by another, this time with the distinctive purple and red logo of FedEx in large letters on the side.

The driver collected a package from the side door of the van, before sprinting up the steps into the building. Why did couriers sprint everywhere? she idly wondered, but then a sudden movement within the building interrupted her thought.

A dark-suited shape emerged from round a corner and intercepted the courier on his way to the front desk. It was a man, that much she could see, although his face was obscured by one of the floor to ceiling transparencies of Coca-Cola employees. The idea, known as the *Glass Quilt*, had started off as a temporary morale booster, but had proved so popular they kept bringing it back, with different staff members and different stories.

Right now it was standing in the way of identifying the person responsible for a whole lot of grief, and she wished they'd never thought of it.

The man in the suit signed for the package and turned to head back towards the elevators. Just at that moment he moved away from the giant photograph and his face was clearly visible, clearly *identifiable* in the focus of her glasses.

Strange, she thought to herself, I never would have suspected him at all.

Three thousand miles away, Fizzer, Tupai and Dennis met a delightful young lady named Kate Fogarty in an Italian bakehouse across the street from a huge, glass-fronted office block which housed Corker Cola Aust. Pty Ltd.

The aroma of fresh bread and cappuccino coffee wound around them as she sat down at the small, wrought iron, marble-topped table by the window, smoothing her long straight hair behind an ear with a casual and well-practised gesture. Outside, the sun had just risen past the side of the Corker Cola building and the early morning rays were washing the table in a rich honey glow. It was a peaceful tranquil morning, with no hint of the dangers that lay ahead.

Kate, she explained, had been Harry Truman's personal assistant at Coca-Cola Amatil in New Zealand, and they had got on well, but she had wanted to move upwards, not to remain a PA for the rest of her life, and he had encouraged her to complete a Marketing/Communications degree part-time. Now she was a rising executive in Coca-Cola Amatil in Australia.

She had plenty of good things to say about her former boss, and Fizzer felt Harry was right to trust her.

'I bought the three cellphones,' she said. 'They're connected and working; I've tested them. The hired car you asked for is parked on the street outside, it's a silver Commodore, you can't miss it.' She held out the cellphones and car keys.

'And here's the cash you asked for.' She handed over a plain white envelope.

Fizzer took it and glanced briefly inside. 'Crikey,' he said. 'There must be a couple of thousand dollars in here. I only asked for five hundred, in case we needed to pay for taxis, or accommodation or anything.'

Kate shrugged. 'That's what he sent.' She looked curiously at the two boys. 'He seems to think very highly of you both.'

Fizzer smiled to cover a small feeling of embarrassment. It seemed that quite a few people were putting a lot of stock in him and Tupai. He hoped they were going to be able to live up to it.

Kate rose from the small table. 'I've got to get to work. Harry doesn't want me to be late today; he said it was essential that I do nothing out of the ordinary. But he wouldn't tell me why.'

She waited for a moment and, when no explanation was forthcoming, said, 'But I expect I'll find out all about it in due course.'

After she was gone, Fizzer rose and said, 'Time for Daniel to enter the lions' den.'

Tupai nodded and pushed his chair back. Dennis said, 'I'll go and find the car.'

They quickly discovered that the huge street frontage and the great Corker Cola sign on the building was just a façade. It was a real office block all right, and it was full of offices, but very few of them belonged to Corker Cola. There were lawyers, accountants, a large firm of civil engineers, a lifestyle investment company and an insurance broker to name a few. Corker Cola, it seemed, paid for just half of the fifth floor, plus the naming rights to the building, which made the company seem to be much larger than it really was.

Whoever designed the atrium had gone in for potted plants in a big way. It was part entrance way and part jungle, with ferns, trees and shrubs arranged in clumps, even a small stream ran underneath plastic floor panels.

Fizzer was nervous, although he tried hard not to show

it. They were walking into a nest of vipers for all he knew, but *someone* had to do *something*, and there really wasn't anybody else.

A brass panel by the lift gave the names of all the firms and their floors and there were a lot of them, so it took a couple of moments to search through and find Corker Cola. Satisfied, they returned to the entrance way and took seats on a long vinyl sofa in fashionable shades of dark blue and burgundy. A rack of magazines stretched along the side of the sofa, and Fizzer picked up a copy of *Time*.

'What now?' Tupai asked, idly leafing through a *National Geographic*. It had an article on the lost-and-found-again Incan city of Macchu Picha, perched high on a mountain top in Peru, and he showed the photo to Fizzer.

'Wait.'

'What for?'

'I'm not sure. But anyone who is going into or out of Corker Cola has to pass through this entrance. So we wait. And watch. And listen.'

Tupai shook his head. 'We can't just sit here and hope that a clue is going to fall over us. We have to do something.'

Fizzer turned his head slowly to look at his friend. 'You could be right. But let's give this a try first. I have a strange feeling that we are right where we need to be.'

Tupai raised an eyebrow for a moment, before nodding and sinking back into his *National Geographic*.

People came, people went. Tall people, short people, thin people, fat people, young people, old people, and a range of ethnic varieties that you would never have seen in one place in New Zealand. Sydney was a great melting pot.

132

The morning passed. So did two more copies of *National Geographic*, a *Sports Illustrated*, a *Newsweek*, and even an *Australian Women's Weekly*, which promised an interesting exposé on the British Royal Family, but turned out to be just a rehash of several stories that had been on the news a few months ago.

Eventually, by rooting around through the piles of old magazines, Tupai found a fairly recent issue of *Pro-Boxing* and that kept him happy through till lunchtime, when Dennis brought over a couple of rolls from the Italian bakery.

Fizzer didn't turn a page. He'd opened it to an article on the US President and that was the page it stayed at the entire time they were there. Fizzer focussed. He made himself aware of the room, every tiny facet of it.

He breathed deeply and recited some meditation phrases under his breath until his breathing slowed and his heart rate began to drop. Then he started to 'pick up' the room. First the walls and the polished marble tiles, the rotating glass door. Then the furniture, every piece, its position, its fabric and construction. The plants, the way the leaves moved in the light breeze when the main door turned, the twisting of the trunks. The position of every leaf on every branch on every plant. The arrangement of the bark that covered the base of their pots.

Once he had picked up the room he was able to discard it, aware of it, but only in the background, like the sound of his own breathing, or his heartbeat. By becoming aware of the room he was able to eliminate it.

Then he started concentrating on sound and movement. Their view was towards the lifts and the centre of the room. No-one could exit without being seen by him.

He concentrated. *He focussed his perception.* He concentrated on the low hum of the air-conditioning until he became fully aware of it and was able to send it to the background and eliminate it from his consciousness. He saw all the people coming and going, he heard them, heard the low conversations about mundane topics, the day-to-day trivia of people on their way to and from work and business meetings.

He could hear the breathing of people as they entered, hear the sound of their watches ticking, the rustle of their clothing. He observed the angle of their heads, the way they held their hands, the young lady, barely pregnant, nervously twisting her wedding ring, the smooth young entrepreneur in the suit that belonged to somebody else, rubbing his thumb and forefinger together as if he had just picked his nose.

He felt the disturbed air of their passage and discerned the mixture of sweat, shaving lotions and perfumes, cheap and expensive, which wafted past.

He listened to snatches of conversation, waiting for a key word that would let him latch on to one of the conspirators. '… told you she was a little poison piglet who …', '… and he emailed it to his supervisor, not realising that she was her aunt …', '… OK then, I'll meet you at the …'

He didn't eat the roll that Dennis brought, and he 'picked up' the sounds of Tupai eating his, so that he could eliminate them from the universe that surrounded him in the spacious well-foliaged atrium.

LOOSE ENDS

Borkin's target went down to the basement car park immediately after the special board meeting. The meeting had gone well, she thought.

The parcel containing her recipe had arrived but, after being switched by her target at the entrance to the building, the recipe shown to the board was a fake all right, but not her fake!

The board had made copies of the recipe, before sending Senior Technician Ramirez away with instructions to brew a batch as quickly as possible for sampling. Before the meeting Borkin had wondered how close it would be. It wouldn't be the real recipe, but it had to seem real.

She saw her target walk past her office at 5:50 p.m., close enough to the end of the day to seem as if he were simply going home. But she knew he wasn't. She desperately hoped he hadn't yet twigged the trap she was building.

She radioed quickly to the FBI team and confirmed the description of the car. They would pick him up the moment he left the car park and keep him in sight, informing her of all his stops. And they wouldn't get noticed. The FBI was very, very good at this kind of work.

Her cellphone rang, and she plucked it out of her handbag tiredly. It had better be important, she thought.

It was. Fraser and Tupai had not arrived back in New Zealand. The flight had arrived, but they hadn't been on it. There seemed no obvious explanation for it. That caused a chill that started in the extremities of her fingers and spread like iced water through the channels of her body.

Anastasia Borkin expressed her distress by using a phrase she had picked up from the New Zealanders.

'Bloody hell!' she said loudly.

Her radio crackled and the FBI had their first report. The target had driven straight to a nearby mall, and used a pay phone in the entrance. He had made a quick call and was now waiting by the phone. She thanked them and put the radio down on her desk.

A pay phone. She mentally played through the possible moves in this chess game. The target must have contacted the kidnappers, and was waiting for them to call him back. The FBI couldn't afford to pick him up at this stage. Not if they wanted him to lead them to the kidnappers. He would just deny everything. Better to play the waiting game.

The FBI would be able to track down the number he had called, and also the number that called back, although it would probably be another pay phone.

Still they'd be able to narrow it down to the state and hopefully even the city, which would give them a good start. She hoped it wasn't overseas, because that would make it twice as difficult for the FBI, as they would have to involve local law enforcement authorities in the country concerned.

Even as she was worrying about such a possibility, a call came through from the FBI team. The first call had been to a cellphone number, somewhere in Australia.

'Bloody hell!'

ON THE SCENT

He finally picked them up just after two o'clock. The first thing he noticed was the perfume, it had a scent that screamed ostentatious wealth, but that, in itself, was no reason to suspect anything. Nor were the clothes, overtly elegant, fashion for people with more money than style. The giveaway was the accents, a nasally New Jersey accent and a laid-back West Coast sound, trained to neutral-American. Two American accents in the foyer of the Corker Cola building: it might mean nothing, but alarm bells were going off in Fizzer's head.

'I don't care,' he heard a scrap of conversation as they exited the lift. Other people were passing, talking, and he had to really focus to isolate the Americans. The man was speaking. 'I'll camp on their doorstep if I have to. I want my money.'

Fizzer silently nudged Tupai. Tupai asked no questions, but casually rose after the pair had passed, and placed his boxing magazine back on the rack.

The woman was talking now. 'They're just waiting until all the loose ends are tidied up. You should be more worried about the call from Atlanta. Something must be up. Why else would …?' The rest of the conversation was lost as they passed out through the rotating door.

Fizzer remained seated until they had turned a corner outside the building, then got up, speed-dialling Dennis as he did so.

'Guy with a cream-coloured jacket, woman in red trousers. We'll follow them on foot, try and keep close.'

They had disappeared into the crowds that were thronging the inner city streets by the time they emerged, and Tupai wanted to race ahead and catch them. Fizzer caught his arm.

'I've got them,' he said, tapping the side of his nose.

Tupai sniffed the air and looked at him uncertainly. 'Are you sure?

'I'm sure.' That Fifth Avenue perfume was unmistakeable.

Wherever they were going, they were walking there, and they seemed nervous, stopping a lot and looking behind them, pretending to admire things in shop windows while watching the reflections in the glass.

It was basic spy stuff out of a thousand cheap novels and old movies, and it would have been laughable if it weren't for the seriousness of the situation.

Whatever they thought they were looking for, it wasn't two teenagers in t-shirts and jeans, and, anyway, they would scarcely have got a glimpse of the pair, as most of the time Fizzer kept right out of sight of them, hidden in the bustling crowd, the congested pavements. He followed them by smell, and it was easy with the strong, distinctive perfume.

Dennis stayed close, circling the block occasionally when forced to by traffic patterns, other times pulling to the side of the road behind them and waiting for a few moments.

It was a warm sunny day and the air was still. That helped the trailing as well, as a breeze could push the scent into wrong directions and lead them up blind alleys, while rain would have brought all sorts of other smells up from the pavements, gutters and drains making it so much harder to stay on track.

When they weren't stopping and doing their comical 'spy stuff', the man and the woman walked swiftly, as if they had quite a distance to cover and not much time. They eventually pulled to a halt in Chinatown, at a long bank of pay phones on the edge of a crowded, bustling, noisy food hall. If you wanted privacy it was the perfect place, as the surrounding hubbub enveloped you like a blanket, smothering you away from any possible eavesdropping.

Fizzer found a free table.

'Go and order something to eat,' he suggested.

'I've already eaten.'

'I know, but it'll look odd if we just sit here and don't order any food.'

Fizzer was conscious that the eyes of the man were roaming the room. He was a dark-haired man, in his fifties, and took no notice of two ordinary-looking teenagers having lunch.

The walls of the food hall were grimy, but the stalls themselves looked spotlessly clean. Posters, in all colours of the rainbow, shouted loudly in large Chinese characters. Above each stall, faded pictures of Chinese dishes were taped to lightboxes that had also seen better days. One flickered nearby, as though one of the tubes inside was trying, and failing, to spark into life.

The seats were hard plastic, for easy cleaning, and the table was polished metal, for the same reason. Even so, the tabletop he sat at had the dried remains of at least the last six occupants' meals, hurriedly wiped over then left to dry.

All this he registered, then eliminated. The aroma of the many varieties of food he ignored, defocussing from his sense of smell and becoming more and more conscious of the sounds that reached his ears. He stilled his own breathing and eliminated that sound. An extended family was arguing in a harsh, guttural Chinese dialect to his immediate left, that too was sent to the background.

Gradually he eliminated most of the hubbub and chatter, including Tupai's voice behind him, discussing, in Cantonese, various dishes with the owner of a yum cha stand. Fizzer had forgotten that Tupai spoke Cantonese, but didn't let the realisation interfere with his concentration.

That left him listening to the whir of the fans above the frying vats (eliminated), the clack and clatter of cutlery (eliminated), the sound of banknotes rustling into tills, and, from somewhere, the sharp hiss of running water (both eliminated). Then, finally, the purp, purp of the digits on the pay phone in the booth on the wall opposite.

It was the woman dialling, and her voice, when the call was connected, came to him in tiny morsels, drifting through the clouds of blanked out sounds in his mind. The sound came opaquely, sometimes muffled, sometimes obscured altogether, but always unclear, as if viewed through distant fog.

He would have heard better if he'd sat closer, but that would also have increased the risk of their being noticed.

He was barely conscious of Tupai's return, or the way he placed the tray of lo-bak-go, ju-chuen-faan, and char-sui bau on the table so quietly as to make no sound at all.

Tupai's bulk blocked some of the sound from the family

next door though, and the conversation on the pay phone crystallised a little more clearly.

The words 'Coke carton' came to him along with 'fake, set-up, and trap', none of which made any coherent sense. The next bit did though.

'... clean (*missed*) fly out to the (*missed*) make sure (*missed*) and kill them all.'

THE AIRFIELD

They talked it through in the car as they tailed the man and the woman through steadily firming evening traffic.

The man, Joe, was driving. Fizzer had picked his name up out of one of their conversations. The woman's name ended in 'andy', maybe Sandy or, as she was American, possibly Brandy or Mandy.

Dennis had already tried the police but they had not seemed at all interested. Either that or they simply hadn't believed him.

No news of the disappearance of the Coca-Cola Three had been made public, so the only hope they had of convincing the police was by persuading them to contact The Coca-Cola Company, and they didn't want to do that unless absolutely necessary, as they didn't know who to trust there.

'If we just stay on their tail,' Fizzer said, 'they'll lead us straight to the missing execs. The three of us should be able to deal with one man and one woman.'

'As long as they don't have guns,' Tupai said.

Dennis said enigmatically, 'There are ways of dealing with guns'.

'You're sure about what you heard?' Tupai asked.

'I didn't hear everything she said, and I couldn't hear the other end of the conversation, but if I had to put a bet on it, I'd

142

say that something in the US has given them a fright and they're going to kill the executives and bury the whole operation.'

'Murder is a pretty serious business,' Dennis said. 'They don't look like murderers to me.'

'If I'm right, they'd be desperate,' Fizzer replied. 'They're in too deep. Way too deep. And anyway, what do murderers look like exactly?'

Dennis nodded. 'You're right, and even if you were wrong, we couldn't take the chance.'

A few cars ahead, the eye-shaped tail-lights of the blue Mondeo flashed and indicated a turn.

'Any chance they've spotted us?' Tupai asked.

'I doubt it.' Dennis was pretty cool about that. 'We've never been closer than three cars away from them, and there are dozens of cars about like this one.' As if to prove his point, an identical silver Holden indicated and moved in front of them.

Dennis turned off, following the Mondeo at a safe distance.

Fifteen minutes later the car turned into a long, straight lane leading to a small airfield. Dennis drove past, picking up the name of the airfield from a sign, and got busy on his cellphone. By the time they had allowed some breathing space and doubled back to the lane, he had hired them an aeroplane.

'It's a twin-engined Piper Cherokee,' he told them. 'Flies like a rocket; we'll be able to keep up with anything in that, as long as it isn't a jet. They want cash though. Do you have enough?'

Fizzer nodded, and didn't feel at all guilty about spending Coca-Cola money. They were on Coca-Cola business after all.

The sound of Joe and 'Andy's' plane was still lingering around the dusty hangars and offices of the charter plane firm as Dennis handed over quite a large stack of Harry Truman's private money. While filing his own flight plan in the firm's log-book, he had a good look at the flight plan of the plane that had just left.

'They've filed for Brisbane,' he said, as they went through pre-flight procedure in the small cabin of the Cherokee. 'But I bet that's not where they're going. They'll veer off at some point to their real destination. They have a single-engined Cessna. We'll be able to overhaul them easily in this little baby, but we'll hang back, pick them up on radar and wait to see where they land.'

'We don't want to alert them,' Fizzer mused. 'But I guess after they land they'll lose their own radar.'

Tupai said, 'We need to be close enough behind them so we can stop what they're going to do!'

'It'll be tight,' Dennis said, and they were both glad they had him along. He had an air of confidence, of being able to deal with any situation.

The sleek white aircraft took off into the sunset with a throaty roar from its twin engines.

They didn't speak for most of the flight, there was little to say. They had no plans, and there were none to make, as they had no idea what they were walking into. All they could do was wing it when they got there, and hope they were in time.

'They're turning away from Brisbane,' Dennis said after a while, his eyes on the small radarscope in the centre of the controls. 'Heading for the Gold Coast.'

The plane showed no signs of landing at the Gold Coast, however, and continued northwards and out to sea.

'Interesting,' was Dennis's only comment. The two boys waited quietly. The Cherokee flew up the coast, not following the Cessna's flight out across the ocean.

Only after the Cessna circled around once and disappeared from their radar did Dennis yank the controls in that direction. The small plane banked sharply and the darkened beaches of the Australian coast slid away far beneath them, the gnash of the breakers grinning whitely against the dark lips of the shore.

Dennis had noted the co-ordinates at which the Cessna had disappeared, but, even so, it took them a little while to locate the island.

'There!' Fizzer called, looking at a smudge of light on the dark canvas of the ocean.

'Where?' Dennis asked. Tupai also peered into the distance, not seeing anything.

'Just follow my hand,' Fizzer said, aiming with a flat palm in the direction of the light.

Five minutes later Dennis and Tupai saw it too.

The light grew steadily brighter until it became a string of bright pearls on a black velvet pad.

The lights of a vehicle of some kind, just two small pinpricks, were tracing a jagged line away from the small airstrip. The Cessna was a child's toy, parked on an angle at the far end.

Dennis brought the small plane in on a satin-smooth landing and pulled it up, just off the runway, beside the small Cessna.

They had barely stepped out of the cabin door when there was a revving engine, and bright headlights cornered them against the plane. There was the sound of car doors and two burly shapes were silhouetted against the lights. The dark outline of a holster was visible on each of their hips.

'This is a private island,' a voice spoke out from one of the shadows. 'You have no permission to land.'

THE ISLAND

Clara Fogsworth thought she should have been frightened. Terrified. But she was oddly calm and accepting of the situation.

There had been sounds of a vehicle above, then a rope and harness had appeared at the bottom of the sinkhole, with urgently shouted instructions to strap themselves in.

'You're being moved to a new location,' Candy, the bitter woman with the sweet name, had called down to them.

But Clara knew it wasn't true. There would be only one reason for hauling them out of their hole and that was to kill them. The story about the new location was just to make them go quietly, so it would be easier for Joe to bop them on the head, or whatever he was planning to do.

Still she went up in the harness, a winch grinding away above her head. Anything to get out of the cave. And she wasn't frightened at all now the end was near. Her life was a job well done, and this little hiccup would not change anything.

Joe shepherded all three of them at gunpoint into the back seat of a Jeep, and kept the gun aimed steadily at them, while Candy drove, cursing like a farmhand, down a bumpy, rock-strewn track leading to the edge of the island.

There was a jetty, and a small motorised rubber dinghy tied up alongside. Moored in the still waters ahead was the dark outline of the *Turtle Dove*.

The large, black shapes loomed ominously in front of the headlights of the Jeep.

'We had no choice,' Dennis said, taking a step towards them. 'We lost all our instruments, and it was sheer luck that we saw your airstrip in the darkness.'

The voice considered that for about half a second, which was twice the amount of time that a man like Dennis Cray would ever need.

'No way.' The voice was emphatic and the man's hand grabbed his weapon. He never got the pistol above waist height. Dennis stepped in close and twisted it out of his grasp in a two-handed cross-over grip to send it spinning out into the blackness beyond the lights of the airstrip.

The other guard went for his weapon as well, shouting, 'Freeze!'

But the word came out as 'Fwurgle' due to his being struck amidships by a runaway locomotive in the shape of Tupai White, who was not only the toughest kid in school, and possibly the world, but also the hardest tackler in the Glenfield Rugby League Under Sixteens. The man went flying back into the bullbars of the Jeep with all the wind knocked out of him and didn't much feel like moving after that.

The first black shape swung a meaty fist at Dennis's head, but Dennis had just completed a marathon kumite fight against one hundred highly skilled karate opponents, and one more

147

was going to make very little difference, especially such a ham-fisted one as this.

He blocked the punch easily and spun round in a high roundhouse kick that snapped the man's head back and lifted him off the ground, flying backwards over the hood of the Jeep.

For some reason the man felt that was an appropriate place to take a nap.

Dennis relieved the other guard of his weapon and, with a look of distaste, flicked that also out into the rocky blackness beyond the lights.

'We'll borrow their Jeep,' he started to say, but there was a shout from the small shack which served as some kind of office cum control tower for the airstrip, and a pistol shot echoed out into the warm air of the night. Then another.

Fizzer had no idea if the bullets came close or if they were just firing into the air, he couldn't see in the darkness, and there were no convenient puffs of dust around their feet the way there are in the movies.

They just ran. Terrified.

Bing stumbled and almost fell, but Clara caught his arm just in time. They were scraping their way down a rock-strewn path towards the jetty. It would have been a tough track for three young triathletes in the full light of day, she felt. For the three of them, at night, with Joe shouting at them to hurry up, it was a minefield of rocky knobs and edges just waiting to grab them by the ankles and throw them down the steep drop to their left.

Gunshots sounded from the other side of the island, where an alien glow lifted up to the heavens from bright lights of some kind. They had seen a small airstrip on the helicopter flight in, which Clara guessed was the cause of the glow.

The cause of the gunshots was less clear, but it certainly seemed possible someone had come to their rescue. She wondered if it was the police or the army. She didn't know if the gunshots came from revolvers or rifles, or whether the kidnappers or the rescuers fired them.

'Hurry it up,' Joe said again, trying to sound angry but only succeeding in sounding scared.

Scared was good, Clara thought, and, for the first time, she felt she might possibly survive the evening's adventure.

Fizzer and Tupai are two of the bravest people you are ever likely to meet, and Dennis Cray climbs mountains and scuba dives in underground rivers, so he's no limping lily either, but when bullets are flying at you out of the darkness, you don't stick out your chin and puff up your chest and say, 'give us your best shot,' because their best shot is likely to hit you in your puffed-up chest and punch your clock, as they say.

'Get out of the light,' Dennis shouted.

So they ran, scrambling over ragged volcanic rocks that tore at their legs in the darkness.

A couple more shots crashed out from near the shack, and there were voices, at least three of them.

Fizzer located Tupai and Dennis by the sound of their breathing and led them behind a small stand of stunted trees struggling for life in the pumicy soil. His eyes quickly adjusted to the darkness, and he could discern shapes of rocks and small shrubs. The others seemed totally blind.

'We've got to get to the executives before they …' He stopped as another shot sounded and there was a corresponding crack from a rock nearby.

'We can't …' Dennis began, but Fizzer hushed him urgently. Another sound had intruded.

'Listen,' he said.

The sound swelled and they heard it also. The low rumble of diesel engines on the far side of the small island.

'That's how they're going to do it,' he whispered. 'They're going to take them out to sea where they can dispose of the bodies.'

There was a shocked silence, broken only by the shouts of their pursuers and the sound of the Jeep being driven slowly around the edge of the airstrip, its headlights on full beam probing the darkness beyond the landing lights.

'You two stay here,' Dennis whispered. 'Give me a few minutes then throw a few rocks around, make a little noise. After you hear a bit of a commotion, make your way as fast as you can to the boat.' He paused for a moment, then said, 'Don't get shot.'

That sounded sensible.

'Where are you going?' Tupai wanted to know.

'To earn my fifth dan,' Dennis grinned and disappeared into the blackness.

Even Fizzer couldn't hear him making his way among the rocks and crags of the island.

Shouts and the occasional shot carried clearly through the evening air, rising above the idling throb of the engines on the small ship, now brightly lit with floodlights fore and aft.

Candy sat in the front of the small rubber dinghy, holding the gun as if it were a small dead animal she'd found under the shed. It was pointing the right way though, or the wrong way, Clara supposed, depending on your point of view. Joe sat at the back, behind the three of them, revving the outboard motor while a V-shaped wash spread out from the back of the boat, lapping against the legs of the jetty as it slid away behind them.

It was a short trip to the *Turtle Dove*, and still there were no running footsteps back on the shore. No searchlights from Coastguard cutters, or men in black suits and helmets rappelling out of helicopters above them. Whoever was coming to their rescue was taking their time, Clara thought. Once they were out at sea, their death warrants were surely signed.

The rubber boat bumped into the low diving platform at the rear of the yacht, and a deckhand threw down a line which Candy fastened to a small T-bar on the front of the dinghy. She did it hastily, without lowering the pistol, and without looking away from them. Just a couple of quick loops.

She climbed over the bow on to the diving platform and pulled the dinghy sideways up against it. The gun never wavered, though. Joe clambered out, and Candy passed the abhorrent object that was the pistol to him with a look of relief. Joe climbed a short ladder to the deck and covered them from there, while Candy held the dinghy fast up against the platform.

'Get moving,' she said.

Ralph was first, rolling over the rounded side of the dinghy and rising to his feet on the diving platform, water sloshing around his shoes. He started to climb the ladder.

Bing was next and nearly slipped on the wet floor, but recovered himself just in time, muttering under his breath. That's what gave Clara the idea.

She struggled out of the dinghy, but then deliberately slipped as her foot touched the platform, falling forward and colliding with Candy, whose head hit the side of the boat with a satisfying thud.

'Stupid old witch!' Candy screamed, but the trick had worked, the dinghy drifted away from the platform, and, arms flailing, Clara fell into the gap between the boat and the ship.

Her first thought on entering the water was how warm it was, all things considered. Her second thought concerned sharks.

She floundered, she screamed, she grabbed the rope that led to the dinghy and thrashed around in the water with it.

If they had known that she had been a regional champion swimmer in her youth, or that she still regularly waterskied and scuba dived, they might have suspected something was amiss. But, as it was, the crew of the boat only saw what she wanted them to see, a helpless little old lady floundering in the ocean.

The ship's engines, which had just started to swell with noise, abruptly shut down again, there were shouts from above, and a life-ring splashed down near her. She conveniently ignored it.

Then there was a splash somewhere nearby, and two strong arms in a white uniform found her and deposited her roughly on the diving platform. 'Damn,' she thought. She'd hoped to use up much more time than that. She only hoped that the second part of her plan had worked.

As she was assisted up the ladder she looked down, and saw it had. Well away from everyone's attention, the little rubber dinghy bobbed away from the ship, the gentle swell of the waves pushing it back towards the shore.

They counted under their breaths to a hundred and twenty, counting the kids' way, one-banana, two-banana, three-banana, four …

'Do you think he'll be OK?' Tupai asked.

Fizzer smiled to himself. 'They don't just hand out fourth dan black belts in cereal packets,' he said, and tossed a few small rocks as far as he could into the distance. They made a satisfying 'tick' noise as they landed.

That caused some shouts and general alarm amongst the guards so Tupai let go with another handful; his flew even further, drawing the guards down towards the other end of the airstrip.

There was a muffled thud then, and a half-shout, followed by a crack and the slam of a car door.

'Follow me,' Fizzer whispered hoarsely, and they scrambled away from the patch of trees and slipped deeper into the darkness of the depths of the island.

Tupai, behind, could barely make out his own hand and could scarcely believe how Fizzer was able to navigate, as if by some built-in radar, around the dangerous, knife-edged boulders of the island. He followed his friend closely, stepping where he stepped, ducking where he ducked, but, even so, he managed to collect some mighty bangs and gashes on his shins, and one or two on his forehead.

They mounted the brow of a low crest, and a small lagoon lay before them, illuminated by the lights of a ship moored just offshore. Some people were climbing out of a dinghy on to the back of the ship, but it was too far away to make out who they were.

Fizzer and Tupai started down the slope towards the lagoon, very conscious of the decreasing window of time they had. If the ship turned out to sea, then everything was lost.

There was a faint cry from the ship and one of the figures, a woman, lost her balance and toppled backwards into the water.

They could see her floundering and thrashing around near the rubber boat. Fizzer, who was setting the pace, did not slow. A man in a cap, probably the captain, and a few deckhands were looking down from an upper deck, and, after a moment, one of the hands climbed the handrail and dived into the water near the stern.

Fizzer and Tupai had reached a sharp, steep, little path that led down to the jetty by the time Clara Fogsworth was deposited, wet and worried, on the platform at the back of the *Turtle Dove*.

They slipped and slid down the path and reached the base of the jetty, only to hear the muted throb of the ship's engines turn into a mutter and see the bow of the ship cut small breakers in the water as it started to head for the open sea.

'Now what?' said Tupai.

Fizzer said, 'Look,' pointing at the ocean between them and the ship.

Tupai looked but could see nothing.

THE SPY WHO CAME IN FROM THE COCA-COLA COMPANY

Anastasia Borkin was looking at the report in her hand, quivering with fury and excitement. How could they be so stupid? So inept! And yet how close were they to finding the Coca-Cola Three?

The Australian police had contacted Coca-Cola Amatil in Sydney with a report of a kidnapping and suspected murder plot. They'd received a cellphone call and thought it was a hoax and so they had not assigned it any priority, but, eventually, an officer had followed it up and made some phone calls.

By sheer luck, the officer had contacted a public relations officer at Amatil named Kate Fogarty. She had put them in touch with one Harry Truman, in New Zealand.

Harry had subsequently phoned Borkin directly, and the conversation had started with, 'Heaven help me if I am wrong, but you're the only one I think I can trust.'

And so, by a combination of luck and circumstance, the news of Dennis's frantic call to the Sydney police had made its way to Borkin. If it had gone elsewhere, she knew, there would have been a very different result.

She alerted the FBI, and they had made contact back with the Australian police, who, suddenly realising the extent of what they were dealing with, had mobilised a huge task force.

They had traced the cellphone that Dennis's call had come from, and tracked its location using cell site transmitters.

That had led them to a small airfield on the outskirts of Sydney, which in turn explained the subsequent rapid cell site hopping that the phone had made. The phone was clearly in a plane that had flown up the coast of Australia.

The last cell site connection had been from Port Douglas, in North Queensland, then contact had been lost. That could only mean the plane had turned out to sea. An Air Force Hercules aircraft had already been mobilised to search the area.

Two police cutters were already there, and were about to be joined by a ship from the Coastguard. Rescue helicopters and a ready-reaction force from the Australian SAS were on stand-by.

The problem was, 'out to sea' covered a very big area, thousands of miles of ocean and small islands stretching into the heart of the Pacific. The plane had a good range, and could have made it all the way to the Fiji islands if it had wanted.

So they searched, and they prayed. And so did Anastasia Borkin. There was nothing more she could do from Atlanta, Georgia to help the Coca-Cola Three, nor the two brave boys, who had somehow latched on to their trail and, having failed to get any assistance from the authorities, had launched some harebrained rescue attempt of their own. There was nothing more she could do to help apprehend the kidnappers either.

That just left her with the spy. But she had plans for him.

COLLISION AT SEA

It was ironic, Clara thought, the amount of trouble they'd gone to, to save her life, just so they could kill her. Through the windows of the forward lounge she could see two crew members on the very tip of the bow, scanning the water anxiously. The water glowed ahead of the boat, lit by intense underwater spotlights.

She knew a little about boats, and she also knew a little about lagoons. Such knowledge came from having led an exciting and adventurous life. She knew they'd be watching carefully for coral reefs as they gingerly picked their way out of the labyrinth of the lagoon. She also knew that the depth sounder was next to useless in waters such as these, where the bottom could be perfectly flat one minute, then shear up in a jagged, hull-crushing spear of reef the next.

No wonder the two crewmen were studying the water with such intense concentration.

She would have bet any amount of money that the captain of the yacht was furious at having to take the ship out of the lagoon at night, when the reefs would lie hidden beneath the inky waves. But captain or not, he was obviously under orders from higher authorities, and so the boat picked its way slowly through the water.

There was an abrupt shout from one of the lookouts, and the boat shuddered into reverse. The sudden slowing was enough to tip Clara forward out of her seat, had she not caught herself with a quick grab at the arm of the sofa.

One of the interesting things Clara knew about boats had to do with the propellers, more correctly known as screws. Older ships had huge solid screws that turned in one direction when the boat was going forward and the opposite direction when the boat was reversing. In order to reverse the boat, the screws had first to be stopped, before they could start to turn backwards.

But the newer controllable-pitch screw always turns the same way. It is the blades of the screws themselves that change, swivelling on a shaft and turning forward thrust into reverse thrust in a few seconds, rather than a few minutes.

If the *Titanic* had had controllable-pitch screws, it might never have hit that iceberg, but of course they hadn't been invented at that time.

The effect on board the *Turtle Dove*, which did have controllable-pitch screws, was like a car slamming on its brakes.

The boat began to reverse, and Clara's thoughts turned again to rescue, although, by now, it seemed that it was all going to be a little too late.

Fizzer didn't wait for the dinghy to wash up on the shore, but ran out along the end of the jetty, diving into the water and pulling the boat close by the rope that ran through small loops around the outside.

The ship was gliding away, slowly though, which seemed strange to Fizzer who knew very little about ships and reefs, despite having led an exciting and adventurous life of his own.

Tupai also raced out along the jetty and leaped into the boat as soon as Fizzer had it alongside. The boat almost bent in two under his weight, but it held together, and by the time Fizzer had clambered aboard, Tupai had wrenched the little engine into life.

Fizzer steered, Tupai knew even less about boats than he did. The bow rose as the dinghy surged through the water towards the brightly lit ship beyond.

Overhead, Fizzer thought he heard the drone of an aircraft, and glanced upwards for a moment, but there were no lights to be seen in the sky.

They caught up with the ship within a few short minutes, thanks to its slow pace, and Fizzer eased the dinghy up to the small platform at the rear. A loose rope trailed through the water behind the ship, no doubt the line that was supposed to have secured the dinghy.

A bright searchlight was probing the waters in front of the ship, and all attention seemed concentrated at that end of the vessel, which was lucky for them at the stern.

Tupai stood in the rocking dinghy and stretched out a leg on to the platform. He was standing like that, straddling the side of the dinghy, when the ship suddenly went into reverse. The dinghy smashed into the side of the ship and propelled Fizzer forward, rolling him over the bow of the dinghy on to the platform and slamming him into the flat side of the ship.

Tupai was not so lucky. He careened off the side of the platform and went flying backwards into the water beside the dinghy, which lurched away into the darkness.

Fizzer hauled himself to the edge of the platform, peering down into water as impenetrable as a sump tray full of old engine oil.

He wanted to shout out 'Tupai!' but stopped himself, knowing it would do no good, and would only draw attention to him. All he could think about were the big propellers that he knew were down there somewhere, and he didn't have to know a lot about ships to know that if they were reversing, then those blades would be sucking in everything in the water behind them. Which had to include Tupai.

He stayed there, hoping against hope, long after the time passed that Tupai would reasonably have been expected to surface. Despair, blacker than the water around him, crept over him then, and he almost didn't feel the boat hook that jabbed him in his left shoulder.

When he turned, though, he saw the pistol.

THE FAX

Borkin waited by the fax machine until all the pages had slid out the bottom into the plastic holding tray. There were over a hundred pages, but all the vital information was summarised in a few notes on the very first page. She stayed there, giving the evil eye to anyone else who tried to use the fax, until all the pages were through. Harry Truman and Mohammad Sarrafzadeh were nothing if not thorough.

Then she telephoned the rest of the board, calling another emergency meeting. It was time to let them know what was going on.

The mechanical organ-grinder in the corner of the room had accusing eyes as she sat and waited, watching their faces as they trooped in. Even now, she thought, there was no trace of concern or guilt on the particular face she was looking at. Maybe he was a very good actor.

When they were all seated she said, 'We think we're close to locating Bingham, Clara and Ralph.'

There was a murmuring, but she continued quickly. 'We don't yet know if they are alive or dead.'

That brought an immediate hush. She said, 'Australian police are closing in on the kidnappers as we speak, and I'm sure you'll all join me in praying for the safe return of our colleagues. Of immediate concern to me is the fact that one of our own has been largely responsible for the situation we now find ourselves in.'

'That's ridiculous!' Ricardo blurted out, but her stare told him to shut up and sit back down, and he did.

'It's not ridiculous, it's fact. Sad, terrible, almost unbelievable, yes, but fact. Treachery, treason, call it what you will, it is a vile poison.'

'If you're accusing someone in this room, I hope you have some proof,' Reginald said with a grandfatherly concern in his voice. 'This is a very serious accusation.'

Borkin dumped the fax on the table, all hundred pages of it. 'I have plenty of proof, all circumstantial, but enough for me to be sure. Included in these documents is a list of the shareholders of Corker Cola Australia. A very good man in New Zealand did some research for me, well, actually he did it for young Fraser Boyd, but he has passed the results on to me.

'There are no employees of Coca-Cola amongst these shareholders. But when you start checking into family records, sons, daughters, wives, especially ...' she paused for effect, 'wives under their maiden names, then a picture starts to develop. Then we have FBI videotape of a member of this board making a call from a public phone box.'

'That's no crime,' Ricardo remonstrated.

'No,' she conceded, 'but when the call was traced to Corker Cola Head Office in Sydney, then it looks more than a little suspicious. The FBI certainly think there is enough evidence to lay holding charges.' She smiled sweetly. 'And they expect to lay more serious charges once they've had a little chat with the kidnappers.'

There was a long, long silence, during which everyone around the table stared at everyone else around the table, waiting for a sign, hoping against hope that Borkin was wrong.

'Ricardo,' she turned to the swarthy man, who looked more surprised than anything. There were gasps from around the table. 'Ricardo, I don't want to make a scene, so I've asked Special Agent Costello and Special Agent Johnson of the FBI to wait outside. Would you please escort Mr Fairweather out to them? They're expecting him.'

All the eyes at the table turned from Ricardo to Reginald whose face was frozen. After a moment of indecision, Ricardo went to stand behind him, and, after a few moments of the staring and the silence, the accusing gazes, Vice-President Reginald Fairweather, next in line for the Presidency, stood up, white of face, and with Ricardo's strong hand guiding his upper arm, left the room without a word.

Then the commotion really began.

THE TURN OF THE SCREW

The world disappeared with an almighty splash and there was only darkness and silence. Not darkness, well, just for a second, for then Tupai became aware of an eerie glow, reflected off a coral reef below and forward of him, shimmering in the light of the ship's underwater spotlights.

The wall of the diving platform had felt like a sledgehammer, driving him backwards off the boat with barely enough time to grab a lungful of air before he plummeted into the silent dark.

Fish darted backwards and forwards in the glare of the underwater lights. Didn't they sleep? Above the fluorescent ghostly glow of the reef was the black-bottomed hull of the ship. And movement, a slow, lazy, almost hypnotic movement. Around, and around, drawing him towards it. Come here, it seemed to say, come here.

The shock of the impact wore off then, and the movement crystallised into two huge black shapes revolving rapidly in front of him. Scraps of seaweed were being sucked towards the screws of the ship; as was the trailing rope from the diving platform; as was Tupai White.

The rope! He scrabbled frantically with his right hand and it mercifully closed on the loose nylon cord.

The screws were turning faster now and he could feel the

water around him suctioning past into their turbulence. His feet were swinging towards the scything danger, closer and closer. He tried to haul himself up the rope, but the drag was too strong, and it was all he could do to hold on to the rope, with both hands now, his body spinning and tumbling like a rag doll, his feet almost touching the whirling slice of the blades.

Air. He needed air. He had managed a last lungful of precious oxygen before the plunge into the water, but it was not lasting. His throat burned. Why his throat? In adventure books it was always the hero's lungs that were burning when they were trapped underwater.

Tupai's throat burned, his head pounded, his lungs didn't burn, they felt like they were going to explode. Had to breathe in. Had to breathe in. Couldn't. All around was just water. Breathe in water and you wouldn't even be allowed a final scream as you died. Let go of the rope. Let go and it will all be over, quickly, no more burning, no more pounding, no silent watery scream.

The rope slipped in his grasp, and he jerked even closer to the spinning blades. But something was different now. The blades were still spinning but the pull was less. Less. Then no pull at all.

He tried to kick with legs made of jelly and made no progress. He tried to pull himself up the rope but his fingers were so tightly locked that he could not prise his own hands open.

Then, miraculously, came the thrust of water from the screw, pushing him away. We don't want you any more, it seemed to be saying. Go away!

His head broke the surface about five metres from the back of the ship and he had time for just one rasping, beautiful, salt-laden breath of air before the rope snagged tight and pulled him back beneath the surface in the wake of the ship.

He hauled himself up in the water, raising his neck, facing away from the ship and lifting his mouth clear of the ocean. Great heaving gasps now, the sweetest, purest air in all creation. The ship was picking up speed, having found the passage; it was heading for open sea.

Tupai began to slowly haul himself up the rope towards the ship.

'Who is he?' Joe snarled again, waving the pistol a few inches from the faces of Messrs Statham, Winkler, and Ms Fogsworth.

'Who are you?' he turned his attention to Fizzer, not waiting for an answer from the other three.

'Who else is aboard?' He was full of questions this chap and not polite enough to give you a chance to answer.

'He's alone,' Candy said calmly, sitting in an armchair at the front of the lounge and picking at her nails with the end of a letter opener. 'They've searched the ship.'

'I think he's that kid that Reggie told us about. If so, he had a mate.'

'If he had a mate,' Candy pointed out, 'he's still back on the island.' A thought struck her. 'Or somewhere out there on the ocean. Or under it.'

The way she smiled when she spoke cut a shiver to Fizzer's heart. *Or under it.* That was exactly where Tupai was.

'So what now?' Joe asked obtusely. Even Fizzer knew the answer to that question.

'So there'll be four burials at sea tonight, instead of three.'

'Burials!' Bing was shocked. 'You said you were taking us to a new hiding place.'

166

'So I did,' Candy smiled sweetly. 'Well, they won't find you there now, will they?'

Joe said, 'Not with all the lead weights strapped around your wrists.'

The captain entered then, a surly thin-cheeked man with the nose of an Egyptian.

'We're clear of the atoll. And we're picking up a lot of activity on the radar. There are at least two planes in the area, and two fast cutters moving in from the south.'

'Then we'd better get this over with,' Candy said. 'Get rid of the evidence.'

She had once been a pleasant woman, Fizzer decided, but any last vestiges had now gone, sucked into the madness of her bitterness, her disillusionment with life. No sane person could sit there picking her nails and talking about murder with such calmness. Even Joe looked quite sick at the idea, and the captain turned abruptly and left, as if he wanted no further part of what was going on.

They were marched to the stern of the ship, just above the diving platform; the place where Tupai had disappeared.

'Who's first?' Joe asked, waving the gun over the three of them. If the others had been Tupai and Dennis, or Jason and Flea, Fizzer thought, they could have rushed Joe. He'd get one or maybe two of them before they got him. But the others were not fit, young and fast. Quite the opposite. If they tried to rush Joe he'd put a bullet into Fizzer first, then pick off the rest one by one.

Maybe that would be better, Fizzer thought, than the dreadful, tearing lungs of water that would await them at the bottom of the ocean. Still something held him back, something that he couldn't explain. And it wasn't anything mysterious or psychic. It was just the subconscious connection of seemingly unrelated facts, forming a conclusion for which he had no obvious rationale. Maybe it was the rope, he decided much later, or rather *the lack of a rope*.

'Who's first?' Joe repeated. Candy aimed one freshly picked finger at Fizzer.

'Him,' she spat. 'He's the most dangerous, and I don't like him.'

Which Fizzer thought was a bit unfair, considering she had only just met him.

'Get down on the platform,' Joe said, a bit uncertainly, as if he had rehearsed this in his mind, but was a bit more hesitant at putting it into practice.

'Why?' Fizzer asked. 'You're just going to kill me anyway, why should I help you?'

'Get on the damn platform,' Candy shrieked, then a bit more calmly, 'and Joe will put a nice, clean bullet in the back of your head before he pushes you over the side. Otherwise,' she looked at him with a grin that said maybe she preferred this alternative, 'he'll shoot you in the knees, and you'll scream all the way down. But no-one will hear you except a few fish, and maybe some sharks. Get on the platform.'

Put like that, it seemed like an offer too good to refuse. Fizzer slowly lowered himself on to the platform.

'Put your hands behind your back,' Joe snarled.

Heavy handcuffs clamped around his wrists, too heavy. He couldn't see it but could feel that there was something attached to the chain of the handcuffs. A lead weight perhaps, or a length of chain. When he went over the side, one thing was for certain, he was going straight to the bottom.

Footsteps on the ladder behind him. Perhaps if he whirled around and head-butted …? Too late. The cold circle of the muzzle of the pistol pressed against the back of his neck.

'Goodbye,' Candy smirked from up on the deck. Fizzer closed his eyes. And so he didn't see the huge black arm that reached up out of the depths of the water and gripped Joe's ankle in a vice before pulling him, pistol and all, into the welcoming embrace of the sea.

He felt the shove on his chest, though, that flattened him on to the platform, away from the edge, as a monster from the deep spurted from the water and raged up the ladder of the ship. Deckhands came running at Candy's piercing scream, but Tupai knocked them aside like insects, splashes and shouts erupting as they hit the water off the sides of the boat.

The captain emerged from the bridge, another pistol in his hand, and he didn't want to hand it over. Tupai had to break his wrist to take it off him.

Joe emerged, choking and floundering, from the ocean at the back of the boat, his gun on its way to the bottom, along with the key to the handcuffs.

It took Tupai nearly an hour to hacksaw through the heavy chain of Fizzer's handcuffs, while Clara Fogsworth kept the captain's pistol pointed steadily at Candy, Joe, and the rest of the crew, and, during which time, a Hercules aircraft passed low overhead.

Shortly afterwards the massive glare of a helicopter 'Night Sun' spotlight illuminated the ship from above.

EPILOGUE

The rest of the story Fizzer and Tupai told their friends at school, sitting in a circle on the top field. Dennis was there too, and just as well, or they might have thought that Fizzer and Tupai were making parts of it up.

There were four guards, it turned out, on the island, not counting the two who were dozing against the Jeep. All of them were armed. But Dennis struck like a cobra out of the darkness, and it was all over in a few seconds.

The guards had had no idea what was going on, or even that there were people living in the sinkhole. Their job was just to guard the airstrip and the perimeter of the island against intruders.

They were all arrested anyway, but finally let off, and, in a strange twist of events, one eventually got a job as a night watchman at a Coca-Cola warehouse in Perth.

The captain and the crew of the *Turtle Dove* were not so lucky. They were parties, however reluctant, to kidnapping and attempted murder, although their sentences were relatively light.

Candy and Joseph were tried together and treated equally on all charges, despite Fizzer's testimony that Candy was the ringleader.

There was silence in the courtroom as the two Americans were sentenced. This judge was not as lenient as the first, and the sort of activities they had undertaken on Australian soil were not to be tolerated.

Candy will need a few more facelifts when she finally gets out of prison, and the only soap opera Joseph Sturdee will be involved with, is if he starts singing in the prison shower.

Speaking of singing, they both sang like canaries, and Reginald Fairweather was charged with Accessory to Kidnapping, Fraud, and a whole list of other charges. Many people wondered why he did what he did, but he had waited twenty years for his turn at the top, and had simply tired of waiting. The result was a prison sentence only slightly shorter than that given to Joe and Candy.

Anastasia Borkin was rewarded with a substantial pay rise for her part in the rescue of the Coca-Cola Three and, a few months later, was promoted to Vice-Chairman of the company, when Bingham Elderoy Statham the Third retired from the position so that he could spend more time with his third wife.

Corker Cola Aust. Pty Ltd. repeatedly denied knowing anything about the affair, although they admitted receiving a copy of the secret recipe from Candy and Joe.

They were eventually charged under, of all things, the Privacy of Information laws, a kind of an Industrial Espionage. But it made no difference in the end, as, even in Australia, the fury against Corker Cola was huge, and they were out of business within six months.

Coca-Cola came clean with the American public and, as Vice-President Borkin had predicted, the backlash against the backlash was immense. The attack that had occurred on an

American institution was considered a crime against America itself and, once it was shown that Coca-Cola were the victims not the perpetrators, the public outcry in their support was enormous.

Clara Fogsworth took up bungee jumping and spent quite a lot of time touring the South Island of New Zealand. Sharron Palmer became a bit of a celebrity in the airline industry and eventually retired from flying to spend more time with her young family. She now trains new flight attendants at Qantas headquarters in Sydney and sends Fizzer and Tupai a Christmas card each year.

Fizzer, Tupai, Jason and Flea just kept kicking around together, grateful that life had returned to normal.

Tupai and Jason even took up bojutsu, and Jason, who thought he was no good at any sport, found, to his great surprise, that he was good at it. Dennis keeps threatening, though, along with his new wife, Reiko, to take them all on a confidence-building, team-bonding trip in some huge cave down in Waitomo.

But for some reason Tupai won't have a bar of it.

And that, pretty much, was that, except that Harry Truman, the man with the name of the former US President, sent over another carton of Coke for Fizzer and Tupai. There was an envelope inside the carton also, with a cheque, the exact amount of which is a closely guarded secret.

Not surprisingly it wasn't a carton of the new flavour that Harry sent (although strangely enough, cans of that short-lived version of Coke became collectors' items). He waited until production was back to normal and sent a carton of the original recipe.

The real thing.

'Then I did the Thing... The Thing I did when my side was losing and needed to score. The Thing that I had been able to do ever since I could remember.'

Twelve-year-old Daniel Scott has a powerful secret —
he can run fast, superhumanly fast. When his speed wins
him a place as the youngest player in history on the New
Zealand Warriors rugby league team, it is a dream come true.
But as the game of the season looms, Daniel has bigger
problems to worry about and he soon realises that even
being a league superstar has its downsides.

Available May 2008

'With my power I could do what I wanted.
Get whatever I wanted... Anything.'

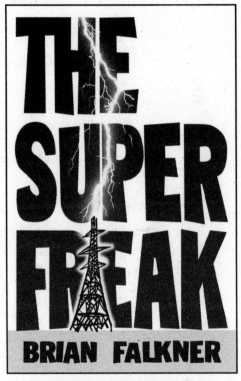

Jacob John Smith is always getting into trouble.
Most of the time, it isn't even his fault — just a case of
being in the wrong place at the wrong time. When he
accidentally discovers he has the power to control
people's minds he thinks his troubles are finally over.
Little does he realise, they are only just beginning.

Available September 2008